VALARAN
CHRONICLES:
BOOK 1

Amalgam

BYRON A.
WELLS

Amalgam

Valaran Chronicles: Book 1

Byron A. Wells

ISBN: 978-0-9880590-7-8

Preface

First the acknowledgements; I would like to thank Natalie, Marta and all the others that helped to proof this book. I would also like to thank my wife and family for their support during the project. Thanks to Reba for the great editing. I would also like to thank you, the reader, for your purchase of Amalgam. I hope you enjoy reading it as much as I enjoyed writing it.

This is a story that expanded since it was first released in 2012; as such, I felt that this volume would benefit from the addition of some extra materials. While not essential to the main storyline, there are three short stories which lend insight to the story and characters: Parem and Ren, which are both prequels, and Abigail which fits among the final chapters of this book. While I could have added the story of Abigail into this revision I thought it better to keep the *feel* of the original release.

Two additional books—I am Archon, and Causality— and three additional short stories will complete the adventures of Hobs and Archon.

Chapter 1

Hobs settled down onto the lush, thick grass that covered Deadmans Knoll allowing the stiff breeze to wash over him, ruffling his loose cotton shirt – he also allowed it to blow away his anger and frustration like chaff in the wind.

He exhaled sharply with a deep sigh as he gazed up into the light viridian sky; he was usually captivated by the vast expanse overhead with its clouds in constant motion. He would lie there and regard the swiftly changing patterns and imagine them taking the form of heroes or villains; characters with whom he could engage in daring adventures – such grand adventures they would be; the tableau could keep him occupied for hours at a time. In the end, and more often than not his endings were good endings, Hobs would save his fair maiden— and then the imaginations would end. "What would happen next?" he often would wonder.

Today, however, was different. Today he simply watched the clouds flow by, allowing the calming beauty he discovered in their swirling patterns to wash over him. From time to time the pale sun would peek through the clouds, warming Hobs and bathing the hill with soft green brilliance. *The warmth of the sun felt good*, Hobs thought as he lowered his eyes in order to survey the landscape around him.

He had never been to Deadmans Knoll before; he had heard the townsfolk tell many stories about the place over the years, yet now that he was here he couldn't possibly believe any of them to be true. It was a peaceful spot, and one that he would likely return to in the future since it almost guaranteed him solitude.

Surrounding his hill to the south and east were dense forests comprised mainly of the oddly shaped Graz trees. No matter how many trees Hobs examined he had yet to find two Graz trees that were alike. Their trunks twisted into shapes and patterns that made you wonder if some giant creature had reached down and shaped them that way. Hobs allowed himself a smile; he had no trouble imagining this giant as he looked up at a particularly foreboding cloud mass; if he squinted just right he could see his giant reaching down to twist another tree.

With a deep breath he inhaled the fragrance of the Graz blossoms that lay heavy on the mid-morning breeze. The forests were in full blossom now; this would mean the town would be harvesting the sap soon – more work. As the result of many hours spent harvesting the sap of the Graz tree, Hobs knew that if you pierced the bark of the tree, it would bleed red blood as if alive.

He pushed thoughts of work aside and drank in the vibrant yellow blossoms set against the dark red bark of the tree trunks. Their broad green leaves spread out forming broad canopies overhead that offered shade from the heat of the day to those who chose to rest beneath them. In many spots the trees drew closer together so that the canopy of branches interlaced to form a dense tangled web. The resulting mesh effectively blotted out the light of the sun and created pockets of darkness in which a person could easily hide.

Many games of hide and find had taken place in these forests that brought thoughts of happier days to lighten Hobs' mood. He had always been good at the games.

He lifted his eyes back to the sky; his memories of better days brought his thoughts back full circle in a roiling turmoil. Just on the horizon, the Jester, one of the planet's three moons, was making his appearance. Peeking his head over the horizon, just a bit at first seemingly checking if it was okay to come out and play. He was visible earlier than usual; It was normal for him to remain hidden until his two brothers, Lumos and Merli, were already well across the night sky.

Hobs wondered if the Jester's early appearance held any portent to what had occurred earlier today, or if *he* spoke of things yet to come. The greybeards of Redwood were oft to say, "The early Jester never sang of any good." Hobs had no clue what they meant; however, he was fairly certain no one else did either. As a result Hobs usually ignored comments such as that and went about his business. They were after all nothing more than superstitious ramblings. Hobs was determined that today would be no different. Turning away from the Jester he effectively shut him out of his thoughts.

Hobs was unusual young man. He was as different from his family and friends as the night was from day. He was born with an inquisitive nature and was often questioning the world around him and the way things worked. He laughed softly as he contemplated what people thought about him—he was considered odd because of his hunger to learn everything he could in regards to the world around him.

The myriad stars that filled the night sky were the sirens that most often sang to him, taunting him with their haunting melodies; melodies that sparked question after question for him to ponder. Among the questions that filled his ears was one that vexed him most—was there life among the stars that filled his night sky? Was there meant to be more to his life than tending grazers for his parochial village?

Hobs brushed his hands through his wavy, raven black hair. It felt silky and clean after the thorough washing he given it last night at the river. He frowned as he considered his hair – it made him stand out. People in Redwood tended to have hair that was either light sandy brown or blond – never black.

As he untangled his hand from his hair, he took a moment to examine it. From the downy hair that covered the back of his hands, to the finely formed fingers that ended in chewed fingernails, his hands were different. Not his hands exactly, he reflected, but the hue of his skin. In a town where everyone had a very slight green hue to their skin he was an oddity; his skin had a light pinkish hue to it. In the past this difference had been embarrassing, revealing with brutal clarity how pale he was when standing next to others. Happily his embarrassment faded away once he started tending the grazers. One beneficial result of being out in the sun each and every day with the grazers was that his skin had attained a vibrant golden brown hue. While still a significant difference from those around him, he was much happier with the result, all things considered.

Standing, Hobs reached toward the sky with a back-popping stretch. Twisting and bending, he worked one kink after another out of his stiff back. He had been lying on the grass far too long and had grown stiff as a result. He was an unusually tall lad; at the age of eighteen he stood head and shoulders over everyone else at six foot four. Redwood was a town where people were lucky if they reached five foot ten. Ever since he had matured he had been taller than his "father," Ren, and his height was a matter that made him more than a bit self-conscious. There was no mistaking Hobs in a crowd of people when he towered above everyone else. On the other hand, it was nice to be able to look down on Roland, the town bully, when he attempted to intimidate him. Roland's cheeks would flush crimson as he craned his neck in order to look Hobs in the eyes.

Not everything was bad in Redwood, he considered as his thoughts returned to Ren—Ren was the rock in Hobs' life and was always able to make Hobs feel safe. Since the age of six when he had been orphaned, Ren had raised him. He had taken him into his home as his son. He owed everything to Ren and hoped to make him proud one day.

Yet he was a young man apart, but no different from his parents. Before they had arrived in town, no one had ever seen anyone different. Ren had told Hobs about his parents and had confided that they had been as different as he, not that Hobs could remember them. He could see the pain in Ren's eyes when he talked about his parents – they had been his friends.

Even if he had been born shorter or if his hair had been brown, there would still be one thing that marked him as an outcast—his eyes. The color of his eyes was a deep indigo blue that resulted in people incorrectly assuming they were black. Lightly scattered through the irises of his eyes were flecks of red. These flecks produced a swirling effect if one gazed into his eyes for too long— the illusion created was so strong that people refused to look Hobs in the eyes when they spoke with him.

Being different meant Hobs was often the victim of bullying and was constantly having to defend himself against the other boys in town. As a result he learned to be quick on his feet; this gained him the unfortunate reputation of being a scrapper and often cast him in the light of being a quarrelsome troublemaker. He didn't start fights, but he wasn't a pushover, he was well able to stand up for himself.

The sad result was that he often found himself alone. As the years slipped by he had become a loner, avoiding contact with those around him as much as possible. Tending to grazers gave him all the solitude he needed.

Grazers – a boring, albeit descriptive name for the majestic animals he tended. They were covered with thick, soft wool, which was used in the production of the clothes worn by the townspeople. They were massive beasts perched atop six muscular legs with broad shoulders giving them the appearance of being barrel-chested. Hobs was the only person in Redwood who stood taller than the grazer's shoulders, which were measured at an average of eighteen hands, and even that was just barely. Unfortunately, while they offered him the opportunity for solitude, they had one distinct pitfall—they smelled horrible. Hobs made a point to find a quiet spot upwind of them while he tended them.

In spite of being the dumbest things on six legs, grazers remained a valuable resource for Redwood. Their care and protection was a responsibility Hobs took seriously. Grazer meat was tender, with a distinct range flavor. As he thought about it Hobs could almost taste the rich green milk they produced—it was as sweet as honey as you drank it, a delicacy to be enjoyed whenever he could get a glass of it, which wasn't often.

The grazers performed another useful function: They took Hobs away from Roland—unfortunately they also took him away from Lena. Hobs thoughts turned to Lena—what were his feelings for her? Did he love her? If so, how could he ever tell her?

Lena was the most beautiful person he had ever seen. Maybe not so much in outward beauty, but her spirit exuded a sweetness that subconsciously drew Hobs to her. She was much shorter than Hobs, with shimmering sandy brown hair and the loveliest hazel eyes. And her voice – oh her voice was like music to his ears, and when she danced and sang, Hobs could only sit there mesmerized. Yet the more he considered it, the more he realized that Lena was the source of his current problem.

"It's not fair! Why can't I enjoy spending time with Lena?" Hobs question the grazer nearest him as he rubbed the bruises on his face. The pain of the bruises succeeded in bringing his thoughts full circle back to Roland.

The grazer bleated in response as if it understood Hobs' current dilemma.

Yes, Hobs had a problem, but not one that could be easily solved – the problem had a name – ROLAND. His hatred of Hobs resulted from how close Hobs and Lena were. He could trace this hatred back to when they were children. Even then Roland had been a bully; however, he had been infatuated with Lena and had stated his feelings for her, only to be constantly rebuffed by her. Roland had unfairly assumed that Hobs was to blame for her rejection of him. The reality, however, was that Lena wanted nothing to do with him. She could see that he was nothing more than a bully, and that turned her off. Roland was good at hiding this flaw in his temperament from the council and elder citizens of Redwood – the outcome being that he rarely received any chastisement that would have only resulted in strengthening his character.

In spite of her rejection, Roland fanned the flames of his desire for Lena, making the most of every opportunity to express his feeling. Time and again Lena had made it abundantly clear that he was to stay away from her. On many evenings, as they sat by the fire, Lena would confide to Hobs that she wanted nothing to do with Roland.

This morning had been yet another adventure with Roland. He, along with the help of his friends Cades and Piers, had given Hobs a terrible beating.

Why?

They had beaten him simply because he Roland had caught him talking with Lena that morning as they prepared for their chores. Their retaliation had been deferred since Roland would never be so obvious as to attack him in front of Lena. But it was only deferred—there was a lesson to be taught and Roland was determined to teach it. Unfortunately his intended lesson had failed miserably.

The image of Roland's face was still vivid in Hobs' mind – it had turned a bright shade of red as he exerted himself. Roland, his fat cheeks lending to the appearance that his tiny eyes were recessed into his skull, had stood there craning his neck to look up at Hobs. He had huffed and puffed and told Hobs in so many words that he was tired of repeating himself regarding Lena.

Hobs smiled grimly. Yes, they may have bruised him, but he had given back as good as he had taken, and Roland's possessiveness had produced the opposite effect from the one he had intended. It caused Hobs to think about Lena more.

The rustling of the leaves as the wind whispered through them arrested Hobs' attention, returning him to where he was. He had wandered much farther from Redwood than was his norm and the area was new to him. In the cool of morning it had seemed expedient to place distance between him and Roland; that way there wouldn't be another "lesson." Deadmans Knoll had been as good a place as any to hide.

Hobs regarded the hills to the north and northwest of him. No one could explain why these hills had the reputation they did, or why the one he was on was called Deadmans Knoll. He did know that it had something to do with events that had happened so many years past that nobody in the village could remember any longer what they were. Facts had a way of turning to legend, and then from legend to myth— Hobs disregarded both legends and myth, having no place for them. Looking around, Hobs couldn't discern anything that warranted the reputation these hills had obtained.

Overactive imaginations, he thought to himself.

Nothing about these hills led him to believe they were haunted as the townspeople said; they were just different. This irrational fear was good for Hobs, especially with the mood he was currently in. He was here and no one else was around which gave him time to think.

The hills themselves were oddly shaped – their shape was likely the result of years of wind and erosion, carving them into bizarre twisted humps littering the landscape. There was, however, an eerie symmetry about the hills that he couldn't quite place. If not the weather then maybe their uniqueness was the result of some ancient cataclysmic event that had shaped them, but what could it have been? Earth shakes?

The sad thing was they weren't even large enough to be truly considered hills. Though he had never been there, Hobs had heard that the Sonora Bluffs, to the south of Redwood, were much larger than these. Still, people avoided the knoll and surrounding hills due to the stories about them and that was good for Hobs – it gave him time to be alone and think.

The bleating of the grazer brought Hobs' head around.

"You think *you* could do any better against Roland?" Hobs paused as if waiting for an answer.

The grazer regarded Hobs with dull eyes, slightly moist from the breeze.

"What would you do in my place?"

Receiving no answer to his query, Hobs let his thoughts drift yet again. He had a good life. He could both read and do calculations. Many in town couldn't say that so it was something to be proud of.

For reasons unknown his parents had felt that these skills were important. Before they had died, his parents taught Hobs the basics and Ren continued his training. They had done this in private, so Hobs did his best to make sure no one learned his secret. There were many in town that felt education was worthless; they would go as far as to mock those who wanted to learn – Roland and his father were part of that group. This mean it was best for Hobs to let everyone think he was ignorant.

Sadly his parents never had the opportunity to complete his education, and Ren was only able to teach him so much. His parents had died as the result of a plague twelve years ago.

Plague – the word alone sent chills down Hobs' spine. The plague was of such devastating intensity that it decimated half the population of Redwood. The town was still recovering from its effects twelve years later.

"I'm sure you already know this but life's unfair." Hobs continued his conversation with the grazer. "Why did my parents have to be taken from me at such an early age? Ren has done his best to raise me properly – don't get me wrong, he has done an exceptional job – I mean, look at me, I am a productive member of the community."

The grazer bleated in response. Hobs could almost imagine it was challenging his assessment of the facts.

"Well it's true. I am productive, more so than others I can think of." Hobs let out a long sigh, "Why can't I ever get a break?"

The bleating of the grazers changed in its intensity to one of fear and alarm that instantly brought Hobs to his feet.

Eerie, undulating sounds filled the air; sounds which sent chills running up and down his spine. It was a sound he had never heard before yet it sliced through him like a knife—it could only be one thing—things that until now he had only imagined in his worst nightmares—howlers.

After jumping to his feet, Hobs did a quick count. The number wasn't right. Counting again he came up with the same result. Three grazers were missing.

With fingers raised to his mouth, Hobs sounded the shrill whistle that he used to call the herd together. Obedient as they were dumb, the grazers started to gather around Hobs. Two of the missing grazers appeared on a path rounding the north side of the hill—one, however, was still missing.

The sound of the howlers filled the air again; Howlers were the stuff of legends – something you heard of in stories intended to scare young children. These nightmare stories would regale the listener with how a pack of two to three of these beasts would descend from the north and stalk the grazer herds. They would continue by extolling the virtues of the town heroes and how they would rise together and hunt the beasts down. Stories such as these were exciting when you were in your home, tucked snugly under the covers of your bed. Out here it was another matter altogether. Ren had told him the terror that attended a howler hunt; he had told Hobs about his friend who had died in his arms during the last hunt.

Panic threatened to grip Hobs; he was alone and it was likely that he would be dealing with more than one animal. Brusquely he pushed aside his fears; he grabbed his quarterstaff before trotting along the path the two grazers had followed. Rounding the bend he was greeted with sounds of a life-and-death struggle. It was the missing grazer, and it sounded both frightened and mortally hurt.

Hobs raised his staff, testing the balance of the weighted end. He swung it a couple of times before firmly grasping it in spite of the sweat forming on his palms. Steeling his nerves, he moved quickly forward, holding the staff ready in front of him.

Rounding the bend, he came face to face with his nightmare. The missing grazer was unsuccessfully fending off five howlers. The number of beasts overwhelmed him. No story had ever mentioned a pack this large; however, it was far too late for him to turn back now. He had to drive the howlers back or more of the herd might be lost.

The howlers were a quarter the size of the grazer, standing on four muscular legs. They were covered with what looked like short, yet very sharp quills over their entire body. Fangs jutted down from their upper jaw, while what looked like tusks jutted upward from the lower. The appearance gave one the impression of deadly efficiency. These beasts could rip apart whatever prey they grabbed hold of. Their front legs ended in three toes capped with razor-sharp talons. The front legs were significantly smaller than the rear. Hobs didn't require much imagination to conclude that they could likely stand erect if they chose on their massive rear legs. It only took moments for Hobs to process this information as he contemplated what his next move would be. He was confronted with five beasts escaped from his worst nightmares.

The howlers had formed a semicircle around the frightened beast, backing it up against some rocks. Just to the right of the grazer was a hole that opened into the ground, dropping down to what appeared to be a cave. There was nowhere the grazer could go as blood flowed from various gashes along its sides.

He watched in terror as a howler leapt at the grazer, drawing its attention. In reaction, the grazer reared up on its back two sets of legs and struck at the howler, knocking it back with a solid blow. The distraction was enough, however, to allow a second howler to get behind the beast where it raked its talons across the exposed flanks and belly. In response the grazer fell forward so its front legs supported it, and lashed out with the hind set, missing the howler by a hair.

The grazer was in a panic, frothing at the mouth. It was obvious to Hobs that without help it would lose its fight for survival.

"Yeeiiaa," Hobs sprang into action with a scream, not considering the consequences as he charged the howlers.

Raising the staff high, he brought it down with a mighty swing striking the closest howler on the crown of its head. The sound of breaking bone was both satisfying and nauseating at the same time. Hobs barely noticed the blood splattering from the impact, or the quills that had gotten stuck just under the edge of the weighted ring on his staff. Adrenaline was pumping and Hobs knew he had to keep moving or it would end badly for him.

"Get...away...from...him!" Heavy breathing punctuated each word as Hobs danced to avoid a howler.

Quick reflexes saved Hobs from the snapping jaws of another howler as it leapt toward his exposed side. Overextending, Hobs almost paid for his mistake fatally. Recovering quickly, he swung his staff again; the weighted end whistling through the air. The howler that had been the target of the blow evaded the majority of the impact by leaping backward. While the staff missed the Howler's exposed back it did manage to connect with its hind leg, breaking it with a satisfying crunch.

He watched the beast as it moved away limping; it hunkered down on the edge of the fight to gaze at him with piercing, inhuman eyes. Hobs could feel the beast contemplating this new threat that was keeping them from their prey. He could feel the frustration emanating from the beasts and a sense of cold hatred of this new enemy.

"Get out of here!" Hobs screamed at the howlers, swinging his staff in circles in a futile attempt to frighten the beasts away.

One howler dead, one injured, and three uninjured remaining—Hobs didn't like the odds. He moved to his right so that he could fight with his back against the grazer. While this would offer him some protection from the howlers, it put him dangerously close to the edge of the pit. He would have to watch his step.

Squealing in panic, the grazer provided all the warning Hobs was to get as the remaining four howlers attacked. Intent on bringing the grazer down fast, they had abandoned all caution.

Watching in horror, Hobs' eyes followed the largest of the beast as it leapt at the grazer's exposed throat. The sound was unlike anything he had heard before. The ripping of the throat was followed by a gurgle of death as the last breath escaped the grazer's open throat. Blood spewed everywhere as the strong jaws ripped through the fur, hide, and muscle.

Backing away quickly in order to avoid being buried beneath the massive grazer as it toppled to the ground, Hobs felt his leg give way beneath him—he had stumbled on the edge of the pit! Of all the dumb things he could have done, he had lost awareness of his surroundings. He felt the impact as the injured howler leapt and hit him full in the chest, knocking him backward. The ground gave way under his feet, saving him from the brunt of the howler's attack. It was only a small consolation to Hobs as he crashed four meters down into the pit, arms wind-milling in a vain attempt to break his fall.

The last thing Hobs heard as he looked up at the grazer's body partially obstructing the pit overhead, was the sound of the howlers feeding noisily, making him sick to his stomach. As he glanced over the body of the dead howler beside him, its neck broken by the fall, the last thing he saw was a strange, flashing red light. *"What was is it?"* he wondered as everything went dark.

Chapter 2

Ren stared out the shop window, his thoughts a swirling jumble. He loved Redwood, yet as he regarded the buildings around him he could see how the long years wore heavy on the ancient town. Nestled into the Graz forest as it was, the town was spared the harsh caresses of the winter winds that whipped down from the northeast. Winds that were strong enough to knock down trees and any other obstacles unfortunate enough to be in their path.

The town itself was nestled deep in the forest, built within a shallow dell. On the east side of the dell a rocky rise climbed above the forest that formed a natural barrier from the winds. It was an ideal location for the town. Over the ensuing years, the forest had been cleared around the center of the dell allowing for the expansion of the town to what it was today.

The buildings that comprised Redwood were nondescript, made of stone and mortar, none taller than a single story. When they were able to do so, the town builders would incorporate the environment around them in their design, as if to hide the buildings.

Deep in the forest as it was, you could pass by the town and never know it was there. The original builders had constructed the town this way for a reason, but Ren was certain no one could remember why. As far as the villagers were concerned the town had always been this way.

From Ren's vantage point in the smithy he could see the council hall with its back butted against the rocky rise. Its careful construction successfully concealed the cool, dry cave that wormed its way into the ridge. The cave offered a safe environment in which to house the council's Hall of Records.

The importance of the council hall was evident in the way everything else in town had been built around it. Two loose semicircle rings surrounded the hall, each ring offering a semblance of protection to what lay within. The inner ring contained the homes of the townsfolk, their windows opening onto a plaza that was encompassed by the ring of homes. Trade shops formed the outer ring, the backs of the buildings forming a solid wall deterring an invasion by the forest.

On the north side of the village were the grazer paddocks. A "harrumph" escaped Ren; he felt quite fortunate indeed to be on the south side of the village. Situated where he was, he could look down to walkways that allowed access from the outer to inner rings and see the paddocks. The fortunate part was that he didn't have to smell them. In all, there were three main paths that allowed access from the outer ring to the inner—one path each leading to the north, west, and to the south. The town entrance was situated on the west side of the wall; a massive gate nestled in the wall opened onto a wide path that wound its way through the forest to the plains and river beyond.

Ren's shop was the metal foundry. Between his shop and the paddocks were the shops of the other tradesmen. He was considered a good metalworker, which resulted in many commissions from Redwood as well as other communities. These commissions kept him quite busy.

Since the founding of the town, Redwood had been governed by a council comprised of three elders. Ren counted himself fortunate to be a member of the council alongside Jonaton and Pol. Being a council member didn't infringe much on his time. Their responsibilities, while important, were few—providing guidance for the people of Redwood, manage improvement projects, presiding over the equinox festival twice a year with its Ceremony of Union, and on the rare occasions that someone violated the town's rules, they would pass judgment over the accused. They were the leaders and historians of the community, educated and well respected by all.

Membership on the council was a rare honor, bestowed when a council member retired or passed away. The retiring member would select and train his replacement, often grooming them for the position over many years. The fact that his choice would require ratification by the other two members was usually seen as a mere formality.

Ren had been chosen for the council five years prior. His consideration at so young an age spoke well of his character and standing in the community. He had replaced his father, who had sat on the council for twenty years prior to his election. Working hard as an aide to his father, Ren had spent eight years learning the council mandates before being selected.

Jonaton, the senior council member, had heartily endorsed his appointment. Pol, on the other hand, had strongly opposed it. His father's final say in the matter was the reason Ren's appointment had passed. There had to be just cause to reject a retiring member's replacement, and Pol hadn't been able to provide any valid reasons for his objection. In fact, all Pol had succeeded in doing with his interference was create a chasm of distrust between himself and Ren. More often than not, he found himself opposed to Pol's proposals, which resulted in the polarization of the council, with Ren siding with Jonaton in the conflict.

As he watched people moving to and fro going about their business he considered, not for the first time, how Pol had won his seat. He let that train of thought dissipate, carried away on his soft sigh—back to work.

Being both the town metal smith and a councilman kept him busy, but it was his responsibility raising Hobs that was the most disconcerting. Hobs would never truly replace his own son Fre, who had died in the same plague that had taken Hobs' parents, but he loved the boy all the same and tried his best to raise him properly – it was what Parem and Rowena had wanted before the passed. Usually he was very understanding of Hobs; however, Hobs could try his patience effortlessly.

Looking around his shop he concluded that today was no different. Hobs' general lack of interest in the family business was in the front of his mind as he reviewed the pile of commissions waiting to be completed. The metal smith shop had been family-run for generations, and Ren wanted to see that continue. The problem was Hobs' lack of interest in running the business. This lack of interest resulted in Ren being forced to train an apprentice to assist with the shop. The fact that his current apprentice, Piers, was one of Roland's friends did little to lighten the dark mood that had settled over Ren. Roland and his friends were a constant source of problems for Hobs.

While others might not see it, Ren was fully aware of Roland's behavior – he was a bully, pure and simple. However, with his father on the council, there wasn't much he could do about the boy without starting a council war, and that was something that couldn't be allowed to happen – so Ren waited and watched. Given enough time, Roland would make a serious error in judgment and get caught. It was only a matter of time and patience, and Ren was used to waiting.

Knowing that it made no sense to delay his chores any longer Ren started putting his tools away; each one was hung in its proper place. Scowling, he thought it was just like Piers to be absent when cleanup needed to be done; still, the boy was quick with his hands and was rapidly learning the required skills.

Rare were the times that Ren could get Hobs to assist with the craft, but when he was successful, Hobs proved to be brilliant – he was quick with his hands and he possessed a good eye for detail. As he considered Hobs, he realized there was nothing the boy couldn't do when he set his mind to it – but those times were growing more and more rare of late.

There was a distance forming within Hobs, one that was setting him further apart from those around him and Ren was at a loss as to the reasons why.

The boy was different – that fact alone would set him apart from the other lads his age – but that was only a part of it. Things weren't much different now than they had been when Hobs was younger, so what had changed? Ren sincerely hoped it was just a stage Hobs was going through.

With the tools put away for the night, he ran his hands over the edge of the worktable. Even though his fingers were heavily callused, the result of years working the foundry, he could still feel the smooth texture of the worktable surface as his fingers caressed it. Many years of work had been required to polish the wood this finely—work that had spanned decades. Closing his eyes, he could see his father teaching him in this very room.

Over the years his ancestors had toiled in the foundry, perfecting their trade. Now it was his turn to pass on the craft and Hobs wasn't interested. That thought did little to lighten his already dark mood. With a decisive choice, he ended his musings as he left the shop. Closing the door behind him, he removed the heavy key ring from his belt. He selected the iron key for the shop and used it to securely lock the door.

With his work done for the day he turned to head home.

He loved his life here in Redwood and his interactions with its people. These people were his family and friends, and he was able to serve them in the position for which his father had carefully prepared him. It was this same honor that he one day wanted for Hobs. If only he could ground the boy in reality. His mind was constantly in motion—involved in roaming the countryside, immersed in some fantasy or in a vain attempt to discover how something trivial worked. Ren needed him in the here and now, with his mind on the day-to-day tasks that were required of him.

Looking up, Ren noted the position of the sun just touching the horizon. Hobs should be returning with the grazers soon. Night was not a time to wander the countryside alone. If it was just Hobs then he wouldn't be so concerned. He was well able to take care of himself; however, he was responsible for the care of the town's grazers. If a single grazer was lost, the entire community would feel the effect. This precept had been drilled into Hobs time and again, and he knew the boy understood the trust he had been given.

Though they hadn't been seen in years, the biggest danger was the potential of a howler pack making its way down from the north. The last time a pack had been seen was when Ren was fifteen. The men from town had banded together to hunt the beasts, and Ren along with them. His father had deemed him old enough to join the hunt; a tragic hunt where he had watched in horror as his best friend was ripped apart by the pack. Food had been scarce and the howlers had been hungry and aggressive.

While they had succeeded in killing the beasts, the cost had been high. Ren had lost his best friend as well as two other townsmen. The skins of the beasts had been displayed on the town walls for years after until the elements had destroyed them through constant exposure. That hunt would be forever etched in Ren's mind.

Sounds of a commotion thundered from the edge of town. Stopping, Ren craned his head to listen. The sounds were angry and getting louder. Without a second thought he moved quickly toward the source of the commotion.

Working his way through the gathering crowd, he observed the grazer herd huddled just inside the gates, moisture glistening on their fur as if they had been driven hard back to town. However, as he looked around he could see no sign of Hobs. Where was he? He was never neglectful of his duties. Why would he have risked the grazers by driving them this hard back to town?

"The boy has gone too far this time." Pol turned on Ren, confronting with open hostility. "The herd is here but there is no sign of Hobs. We could have lost the entire herd due to his irresponsibility!

Look at them—they're all in lather. Without a doubt there will be no milk from them for days."

A murmur of assent rose from the crowd.

Ren was worried. Something was not right here.

Shouting to be heard over the cacophony of the crowd, Ren yelled, "Let's all settle down."

The crowd quieted leaving only the bleating of frightened grazers to fill the void. "First, are all the grazers accounted for?"

Muted stares greeted his question – no one had thought to check.

"Mick, would you do a quick count please."

Ren watched the young man move to complete his task. "Now, has anyone seen Hobs? Does anyone know where he went this morning with the herd?"

Lena appeared to have something to say but it was Roland, Pol's son, who spoke instead. "I saw him head out this morning. It was just after sunrise; he went northwest, towards the river. He had the grazers with him."

From the corner of his eye, Ren saw Lena fidgeting as she cast a glance at Roland. She appeared on the verge of saying something before a sharp gesture from Roland held her back. Warnings sounded in Ren's head. "You're sure about this Roland?"

"Yes sir, I was just coming back from a quick morning bath in the river and passed him.

"Did anything happen? Was there anything that could explain him not returning with the herd?"

No one laughed as Roland's face contorted; he was obviously thinking hard. The result would have been comical at any other time, but not now. "No sir, I said hi and he grunted a reply before going his way."

A clearing throat interrupted Ren. Turning, he realized Mick had returned. "Any missing grazers, son?"

"Yes sir, I counted twice just to be certain, but we are missing a grazer."

Taking charge of the situation, Pol hijacked the conversation by forming search parties to look for Hobs and the missing grazer. While he appeared determined to find out what happened, Ren was sure that the grazer was the more important of the two in Pol's view. Finding Hobs would be secondary; if he was found, then Pol would mete out a punishment as he saw fit – he wouldn't wait to bring the matter before the council. Jonaton would then rebuke him for his lack of due process but the harm would already be done.

"Are you coming, Ren? He is your son after all..." Pol sneered.

Ren cursed silently for losing control of the situation and determined to find a way to wrest control back from Pol.

"I'll catch up. I just need to get some gear from the shop first," Ren said, making a mental list of the items he needed to gather before he would head out.

With a scoffing laugh, Pol divided those he assembled into three search teams. Roland and his two pals Cades and Piers formed one team. Mick and his father formed the second, leaving Pol to team with Ren when he was ready.

"Meet us at the river when you're done." With that, Pol led the search parties out of town.

"A word please Lena," Ren quietly spoke to the girl as the remaining townsfolk dispersed, returning to their homes.

Lena looked cautiously around before whispering in reply, "I'll meet you at your shop shortly," then scurried off, following her mother to the house they shared.

Abigail was a fine woman who was charged with the care of the younger children in Redwood. She had raised her daughter as best she could after the death of her husband in a mining accident and the consensus of all in town was that she had done quite well. Lena had blossomed into a fine, well-mannered young woman. Ren knew that Hobs was interested in Lena and hoped they could come to an understanding.

Looking toward the edge of town, Ren caught Roland watching him, his cheeks reddening in anger. Something was going on, but what? Hopefully he would find out soon, he thought, making his way back to his recently closed shop.

From behind the counter he grabbed the weighted club that he kept for dealing with wild animals. Next, he grabbed a lantern from the back storeroom, which he proceeded to fill with oil. Rope—you never knew when that would be needed—was added to the growing pile. He grabbed a shoulder bag from the storeroom in the rear of the shop – additional items quickly filled the bag. Once everything he needed was stowed he was ready to go; now he just had to wait for Lena to arrive.

It was nearly an hour before he heard her furtive tap on the door. She entered quickly and quietly when Ren opened the door for her. She appeared frightened which piqued his interest yet he gave her time to compose herself before asking, "Lena, Roland wasn't telling the truth was he? Hobs didn't go northwest this morning, did he?"

Lena slowly shook her head no…

"What happened this morning?" he continued, willing her to speak with his eyes.

Light blond hair fell loosely to her shoulders, framing her elfish face. Tears filled her soft eyes as she answered, "Roland found Hobs and I talking this morning as we started on our chores…he was furious." Taking a handkerchief from her pocket, she lightly dabbed her eyes. "He didn't start a fight at that time; instead he told Hobs to leave me alone. Leave me alone—as if I was his property." Fire flashed from her eyes, the anger clearly evident as she spoke of Roland.

Lena paused for a moment to gain her composure before continuing; "Roland was only delaying the fight since he didn't have his buddies with him. After he gathered Cades and Piers, they went after Hobs. I made sure they didn't see me following them. They caught up to Hobs in the narrows as he was guiding the grazers out to pasture. I watched as they *persuaded* him to leave me alone."

Ren put a comforting arm around her as the sobs started again. "It's alright Lena."

"NO," she screamed, interrupting him. "You don't understand at all. It wasn't just a fight…they beat him. I think they might have killed him if I hadn't stopped them. When he rounded on me, I thought Roland would hit me he was that angry. Instead, when he realized it was just me, he stopped beating Hobs and actually started laughing." Lena looked up at Ren. "Then he and his friends walked away, leaving Hobs there with bruises forming on his face.

"I tried to help him," Lena continued. "I wanted to put some ointment on the bruises, but he just brushed me off saying it would only make matters worse. As I watched him walk away he was leading the grazers northeast, not northwest as Roland stated." She broke again into soft weeping, holding her face in her hands. "I'm so sorry," she chanted over and over rocking in Ren's arms.

Ren considered what Lena had said. Forest-covered hills covered most of the territory north of town; in fact there wasn't much grazing land in that direction until you reached Deadmans Knoll. With its reputation no one went there. Could Hobs have gone to the knoll knowing he would have a chance to be alone? Was he in trouble?

Thanking Lena quietly, he gave her a strong hug providing the comfort the girl needed. He liked her, and Hobs had crushed on her for as long as he could remember.

Rising, he held the door open for Lena. As she was leaving he posed one more question to her. "Lena…"

Pausing, she turned slowly to face Ren.

"Did Roland see which way Hobs went?" he asked quietly.

She paused before slowly nodding her head in assent, tears gently flowing once more in glistening streaks down her cheeks.

"Thank you, Lena," Ren said consolingly as she turned again to go.

He watched as Lena followed the pathway to the plaza. He lost sight of her as she turned toward her house.

He had a destination now yet it was doubtful that he would find someone who would be willing to go where he needed to go; he wasn't about to let that stop him. Hobs was in trouble, he could feel it in his bones. He needed to be sure nothing had happened to him.

Locking the shop for the second time that evening, he quietly headed out of town.

Roland held back as the search parties left town, his curiosity getting the better of him. He needed to see what Ren was scheming. With quick words to Cades and Piers, he informed them that he would catch up with them shortly before sending them on their way.

Hiding in a dark, recessed doorway he was able to observe Ren's shop without being seen. It had taken an hour, but the waiting had paid off. He watched as Lena entered Ren's shop only to leave shortly after.

What had she seen? Better yet, what had she told him?

His father had made it clear that he was to stay out of trouble, and this could present a huge problem for him.

Damn Hobs. There was something about him that brought out the worst in Roland. He had an air of smug superiority that Roland hated.

The closing of a door brought his attention back to the metal shop. He watched Ren shoulder a small pack and head towards the gate. Moving deeper into the shadows, Roland watched Ren pass. Then, quietly as he could, Roland followed him. When they reached the edge of the forest, Roland's suspicions were confirmed—Ren didn't head northwest; instead, he headed northeast following the path Hobs had taken earlier that morning.

Unsure what else to do, Roland hurried to the river to speak with his father.

Chapter 3

Electrons moved swiftly through the circuits, like water running its course. Relays were closed causing alarms that hadn't sounded for centuries to scream to life. These alarms echoed through the vacant corridors of the massive underground facility. Defense systems that had long been dormant were activated in response to the wailing alarms.

This was the home of the ancient Intelligence known as Archon, one of the last remnants of a long-forgotten galactic empire.

Words fitting enough to describe the complex entity known as Archon would barely be able to scratch the surface of the enigma that he presented.

Did you call Archon *he* or *it*? Or did you just call him Archon?

Referring to him as a sophisticated Artificial Entity, or AE, would be simplistic at best yet that was the designation that had been given to him by his Valaran creators during the height of their rule of the stars – during an age when technology had managed this planet.

During the zenith of their rule, the Valaran Empire had spanned thousands of star systems scattered throughout this region of space. A major military outpost was established on Cygnus in order to maintain the peace on this remote side of the galaxy. Archon had been installed in the facility with the purpose of governing Cygnus Prime in the service of the Empire.

The Empire was no more, yet Archon remained. He had been overlooked by the Scarian when they led their bloody revolt against the Valaran a millennium ago. Since the fall of the empire Archon had remained hidden in his underground lair, processing data day in and day out – all the while managing an empty facility.

A warlike reptilian species, the Scarian were once subjugated by the Valaran. However, subjugation by the Valaran wasn't like slaves serving a master; instead, it was the Valaran imposing their guidance over a race that was hell-bent on a path of self-annihilation. If they had been left to their own devices the Scarian would likely have been extinct within a few generations. In hindsight, Archon pondered, leaving them alone might have been for the greater good.

The Scarian felt that the Valaran had defrauded them of their freedom, and that was an unacceptable position. The result was that for the first time in their brief history, the Scarian united under a war council in revolution. It was a revolution to be carried out against their oppressors, the Valaran.

Their hatred had burned so deep that it exploded in a campaign of genocide that resulted in the extermination of the Valaran race. No one was spared from their onslaught as they butchered men, women, and children alike. Their rampage was so vicious that it decimated everything that the Valaran had built – or so they thought.

The only reason Archon escaped this juggernaut of destruction was that his facility had been hidden. Planetary Commander Wrightstone had made a decision to bury the facility housing Archon along with all the ancillary buildings. Engineers had carefully buried the main structures, forming the hills surrounding what was today called Deadmans Knoll. The Valaran had done this long before the Scarian reached Cygnus Prime. With all systems turned off, or powered down to minimum maintenance levels, the facility was not observable from orbit sparing it from the bombardment that followed.

The Scarian had leveled city after city from orbit, determined to leave nothing standing that the Valaran had built. Once the bombardments were completed legions of the reptilian troopers scoured the surface of the planet butchering any living Valaran they found. Those not of Valaran lineage were left alive; the Scarian assumed them to be just another race that had been subjugated by the usurpers. After a full cycle they departed, leaving a shattered planet behind them. The survivors struggled for existence, scraping out any sustenance they could from the ruins of what had once been majestic cities.

As they left orbit the Scarian seeded satellites around the planet. These were intended to guard their conquests for generations to come. Archon's passive sensors could still locate these guard satellites in orbit; as a result he maintained operations at the lowest power levels and waited. And so the long years passed…

Through his sensors Archon chronicled the changes to the planet around him year after year. His neural network extended over the entire planet allowing him to "see" these changes. The years hadn't treated Archon kindly though and over the past hundred years he had identified breaks in his neural net, which resulted in "blind spots."

He had witnessed the mass murder of the population of his planet. He had watched the survivors rise from the ashes of destruction, and he continued to watch their day-to-day struggle for survival using whatever they could find—yet Archon waited and watched.

Over the centuries, communities had been formed and trade crafts rediscovered. Compared to Archon and their ancestors, these survivors were primitive. Though barely educated, as civilized people should be, he observed that they lived happy lives. As the years passed, he watched life slowly return to his world.

Much as he wanted to aid these people, he knew that he had to remain silent, silent due to the satellites in orbit, and silent due to the fact that they would not be able to understand what he was. If he revealed himself before they were ready then the result would be his being worshiped as an oracle by the people. As such, he had to be careful in the aid he provided. Therefore, Archon formulated a plan that would allow him to help the struggling masses.

Archon covertly began a program of sending surviving Valaran among the populace. If they had remained in the facility, they would have slowly died off, and the end result would have been the same— Archon being alone—so send them out he did. They were tasked with intermingling with the population and to work at raising their levels of education and understanding.

Archon set in motion his plan to lend assistance where he could. The technicians and soldiers he sent out were armed not with weapons of war but with documents outlining simple projects to better the lives of the masses. These Valaran integrated with the communities, mingling their blood with the survivors of the holocaust. Over the years, the Valaran survivors had formed councils to govern the towns, introduced education programs, and improved the lives of their charges.

That was many years past and still Archon watched and waited, hoping that one-day the Valaran would return. Three centuries had passed since the last Valaran had left, and the halls of his facility had remained silent—until today—a ghost facility devoid of life save for the silent hum of machines performing their tasks day in and day out.

He scanned the airwaves daily, hoping without hope to hear commands fill the military channels, indicating a return to order. Yet they remained chillingly silent. There were no Valaran fleets remaining; no armies that would come and restore order on Cygnus.

Instead, Archon found that his systems were slowly decaying with age; they weren't meant to last millennia without maintenance and parts for repairs. Archon had done what he could yet in spite of his best efforts some systems had failed altogether.

On this day, however, something had triggered his external proximity detectors. With curiosity, intensified from centuries of inactivity, Archon silenced the alarms. With a thought, he powered external surveillance modules that had been unused for centuries. He issued the commands to sweep the perimeter as he searched for the source of the alarm.

What Archon found resulted in the activation of other systems. His perimeter had been breached; his existence possibly brought into peril albeit by a potentially tragic accident. Sensors revealed a man partially covered by rocks with a dead beast beside him. The man appeared to be severely injured, unconscious, and in obvious need of immediate medical attention. Programming completed centuries ago required him to save the man inadvertently in his care. He would do so with the full knowledge that by taking action he risked exposing his presence to the satellites in orbit. To do nothing would mean that the man would die.

Tracking the monitor upward he observed the remaining howlers peering down over the remains of a dead beast they had recently slaughtered. Taking note of the bloodied staff beside the young man, Archon concluded him to be a shepherd, injured defending his charge. With a sonic burst he scattered the remaining howlers. There was nothing to be done about the dead herd beast at this time except collect it for food processing; the young man was another matter altogether.

Androids long unused were brought online to accomplish the various tasks Archon set for them. With precision they moved to aid the injured man. They slowly removed the rocks one at a time – Archon was taking no chances. Once the man was free of the debris, orders were issued for the androids to encase him in fast-hardening gelplast; this would effectively immobilizing the body so he could be safely moved to the medical unit for further evaluation.

Another android was provided instructions to set control charges that would be used to bring down the walls of the pit around the entrance – the result would be the resealing of the facility. The hole would be larger but that couldn't be helped. It was necessary that he remain hidden. The final order to the androids was to move the body of the dead animal in the pit to the food reclamation facility.

While issuing the various commands, Archon pondered what to do with the injured man. No one was aware of his existence here and nothing could jeopardize that. He considered what the repercussions of helping the young man would be. Would he ever be allowed to leave the facility?

While watching the progress of the androids Archon accessed a plan that he had been working on over the past century—a plan that would lengthen his existence given the right circumstances.

Archon watched as the androids carefully move the man onto a hover gurney and guided him through the facility. It didn't take long before the android transferred the man to the bed in the medical unit. Once positioned, Archon released a chemical to counter the gelplast, leaving an oily substance that sloughed off his body. Maneuvering scanners over the bed, Archon conduced a precise examination—the exam concluded with samples of his blood.

Overall the prognosis did not look good. There was severe damage to the spine, multiple breaks and fractures in his legs and arms, and a few broken ribs—one of which had punctured the right lung. Other than a severe hematoma on his left leg, there were only minor bruises on the remainder of his body. With satisfaction, Archon noted there was no damage to the skull and brain.

He should be able to save the boy, he decided. Scans allowed Archon to set his age at just under twenty standard years—he was entering the prime of his life.

If Archon had been human, he would have done a double take as he reviewed the results of the blood work. Archon sent commands for the cameras to zoom in for a close-up; he needed to be sure.

Could it be?

The plan he had formed years ago would work, he was sure of it now—Archon made slight revisions to his plan and ran simulations against it until he was satisfied with the results; he then saved the file with triple encryption.

Archon examined the injury list again. The breaks in the spine were of the greatest concern to him; they resulted in him placing the boy on life support as a precaution. It was amazing that he was breathing at all – untreated, the break in his spine would result in paralysis from the neck down. Archon issued commands for the synthesizers to commence with the manufacture a special spinal implant. This implant would be utilized to bridge the broken spine and further the plan he had just modified.

Archon initiated medical programs that he sequenced to perform the various medical procedures required. He watched as robotic arms swung into position, their ends bristling with surgical implements that could be brought to bear, and proceeded to operate on the boy. The punctured lung would be repaired first, then the arms and legs afterward—it would be a simple task to repair the breaks and fractures.

With care, an incision was made in the chest. Inserting a tool into the incision, the medical unit proceeded to manipulate the ribs back into place; following the repair to the ribs another tool was used to seal the punctured lung. In all it took ten minutes to complete the repair and seal the chest. Archon noted an improvement in breathing immediately. He observed the rhythm of the heart and was pleased to see it settle into a steadier pattern.

With the repairs to the lung and ribs completed he ordered the medical unit to continue with the next procedure in the sequence.

Laser scalpels moved into position and opened both legs. Starting at the hip, they cut into his legs, working down to his feet—exposing the bones underneath. Care was taken to ensure that there wasn't any damage done to the muscles and ligaments. The medical unit commenced with repairs to the broken bones. The process was slow and meticulous, but in the end, the breaks were fully repaired in such a manner as to leave no signs of the original trauma.

The next step required chemical agents to be injected into the bone marrow. This agent was designed to spread aggressively through the bones, strengthening them against future breaks and distress. While technically this process wasn't necessary for treating his patient, it would be beneficial for what Archon had in mind.

With the legs repaired, Archon instructed the medical systems to apply neural filaments. The filaments would integrate with the nervous system and form a neural network in the boy's body. Once active they would carry signals much like nerves. Archon was, in essence, building a second nervous system. The neural filaments were much more aggressive than Archon expected, integrating themselves into the nervous system as they spread rapidly through the man's legs.

With the procedures on both legs completed, the medical unit closed the incisions. It sealed them so well that no scars remained when the procedure was finished. Archon inspected the work, not bad, considering how many years it had been since the machinery in the medical bay had been used to save a life. If Archon could have, he would have exhaled the breath that he would have been holding—he realized that he had been just a bit worried that something might fail. Subconsciously, Archon pushed those fears aside, dismissing them as irrelevant to the task at hand.

Before moving on, Archon instructed the medical unit to deal with the hematoma. The blood that had collected in the man's thigh was a simple process for the medical unit to deal with. When completed, Archon rescanned the legs and was pleased with the results. There was a solid neural net integrated with the body's natural nervous system, and a reinforced skeletal structure that was almost as strong as the armor casing of his androids.

Archon repeated the same process on the arms. The chemical agent was applied to the bones, repairing and hardening them. The neural filaments that had been inserted into the legs were spreading faster than he had anticipated and were already extending down his arms. Not one to take a chance, Archon added the neural filaments to the arms anyway. Finally, the medical unit retracted its equipment and powered down to a ready state.

Archon reviewed the final scans of the boy. The neural filaments had completed their expansion and completely permeated the body. They had even bridged the severed spinal cord; however, without the insertion of a control unit, the boy would only have limited functionality.

The control unit would process signals from the brain and pass them to the various parts of the body through the new neural net. Since it was "tuned" to work with the neural filaments, the transitions between brain and net would be faster and much more efficient, increasing the boy's natural response times.

Archon had a special control unit in mind for his ward. A query to the synthesizers showed that it would take an additional eight hours before it would be completed. The device had to be perfect or the plan would fail. Since Archon was use to waiting he settled back into the diagnostic routine that had been interrupted by the alarms.

Chapter 4

Ren lifted his head as he peered up through the trees in a vain attempt to determine the time. In spite of the faltering daylight Ren knew he was making good progress but he would feel better if he could determine how much daylight he had remaining.

Grazers were huge beasts with giant footprints and as a result the path they took was easy to follow—that and the plethora of broken branches littering the ground marked their passage. He estimated that it would take another twenty minutes to reach the knoll. The trees had thinned some allowing him to just make out the hills through the trees. He doubled his pace, knowing it would be close to dark by the time he arrived.

Shadows lengthened around him, dark and foreboding. The air was charged with anticipation, the forest unusually silent. Ren would not be truthful if he said he wasn't concerned. Hobs was his son—what would he find when he reached the knoll? Ren cast his gaze left and right as he moved; the shadows had grown so thick that Ren could walk right by Hobs if he was lying injured within them. That was something he couldn't allow, Ren thought.

Pausing briefly, he reached into his bag and removed the lantern. Using his flint to produce sparks Ren was able to light a twig, which he then used to light the wick in the lamp. Shadows fled as the light cast forth by the lamp penetrated the darkness. With a slow, sweeping motion, he peered into the cover of the trees—searching cautiously, he moved forward, hoping to find any sign of Hobs.

As he searched, Ren found himself wondering why Roland had lied and convinced everyone to search near the river. What was to be gained by his misdirecting? Why was he reluctant to send the search teams in the proper direction? The lack of any rational answers to his questions opened avenues of uncertainty; avenues down which Ren's fear-plagued mind freely wandered.

There would be plenty of tracks by the river, Ren knew with certainty, since it was frequent that Hobs took the grazers there. Beside the meandering river they had plenty of water along with the lush meadows that bordered the river providing sustenance. As the only true trackers in the group Roland and his father would be able to "find" whatever answers they wanted.

They wouldn't find Hobs, of that Ren was certain. He was equally sure it was exactly what Roland intended. As the years passed by, Roland's hatred of Hobs had grown; it was a fact, and one that Ren wasn't able to determine why, other than Lena—but was that enough of a reason?

Could this hatred of Hobs extend as far as making sure Hobs didn't receive help if he was hurt? Whatever he was missing, Ren felt sure it was important.

The sound of an explosion split the quiet evening, startling Ren with its strangeness. A fireball expelled the darkness with fleeting brightness before if faded away – a massive boom, with its thundering reverberations, was followed swiftly by the ground shaking under his feet. As quickly as it had begun it was over, leaving Ren to wonder at its source. The light and sound had come from the direction of Deadmans Knoll. He started moving again, knowing that he would find out soon enough what was happening.

Another sound filled the air, a sound that left shivers coursing down his spine from head to toe. It was the sound of his childhood nightmare—howlers. Ren quickened his pace hoping that he wasn't already too late, a cold knot forming in his stomach.

The river burbled as it wound its way past the bank on which Pol was standing. He regarded the azure waters. Rocks jutted from the middle of the stream, white breakers rushing past them. While the water wasn't moving fast, it was still fast enough that a body would be swept downstream before they could locate it.

Lush meadows bordered the river on both sides providing good grazing for the herd. The country north and to the northeast rose in gently rolling hills. In the distance he could make out the northern edge of the Graz forest that surrounded Redwood. It extended to the north and south, dotting the distant hills.

On a normal day this would be a peaceful spot to sit and think but today was not that day.

The path from town ended at the riverbank where it intersecting the Road—it had no other name. If you followed the Road south, you would reach Sonora's Bluffs and the community there. North just followed the river and wound its way into the mountains. Because of the potential dangers no one went that way—that was howler country.

He returned his gaze to the search parties. They had conducted a thorough search along the riverbank and surrounding meadows where plenty of tracks could be found; unfortunately, none of the grazer tracks were fresh. They were all a few days old and there was no sign that Hobs had been there that morning leaving him to question why Roland had sent them this way.

Cursing Hobs, Pol stomped back to join the search. He was getting tired and blamed Hobs for his current predicament—he was out here as night fell instead of enjoying a hot meal in the comfort of his home. All of this effort being expended for a worthless boy whose loss, if something had happened to him, would have little impact on the village.

There was little doubt in Pol's mind that Roland had a future, one that he was painstakingly grooming him for. Unfortunately Roland seemed to attract trouble in the same way that shit attracted insects—it was a simple fact of nature, a cycle that Pol intended to break.

The fact that Roland hadn't yet been brought before council for any of his indiscretions was of little consolation. Pol knew that the only reason for that was due to his quick intervention when infractions occurred. If he couldn't control his son better, it would only be a matter of time until he did something serious enough that Pol wouldn't be able to spin, and then all of his carefully contrived plans would shatter—becoming a fleeting memory. Pol was determined to do everything in his power to prevent that potential future from becoming a reality, *not while he drew breath.*

Pol had grand plans, which cumulated with Roland joining the council. He had already received grudging acceptance of his election from both Jonaton and Ren. The stupid fools had been so easily manipulated—they had no right to lead the community. Pol felt he was above such machinations and tried to properly groom him for the day he retired. Roland might be rough around the edges, but he did what he was told, and that was what mattered.

Not for the first time this evening Pol looked up, seeking Roland— finally, there he was. Gaining Roland's attention, he motioned him over with a subtle wave of his hand. They needed to have a private talk while the others continued with the search.

He waited while his son shuffled over, his friends nearby.

"Roland, is there something you need to tell me?" The silence was deafening as the seconds slipped by. "Hobs didn't come this way, did he?"

Knowing better than to lie to his father, Roland truthfully answered, "No."

"Do you know where he went? And while you're at it, can you tell me why you lied earlier."

Roland's cheeks flushed as they usually did when he was nervous, and he nodded yes, remaining strangely silent.

Another incident must have happened, Pol thought with realization, anger building as he prompted his son to continue. "And…"

"What's the reason for most of my fights, Dad?" Roland's cynicism wasn't lost on his father.

"A girl? You fought over Lena again. What is wrong with you, boy? You can be thick as a rock at times Roland. Keep fighting and I can guarantee the consequences will catch up to you. Move your ass and see if you can find out what happened to him, in the right place this time."

Roland shrank away from Pol's fury.

"Your lie could be disastrous for you as well as for me. Do you ever stop and think about the consequences of your actions?" Pol's disappointment oozed from his voice.

"I understand, Father," Roland replied, head hung low. Looking up, he continued, "Father…I think Lena knows where Hobs went and I think she told Ren. The reason I'm late is because I waited in town until he left. Lena spoke with him and when he left town he was following the path Hobs took this morning."

"You need to fix whatever this issue is, and quick!" Pol said, turning his back on his son dismissively.

Roland bore holes into his father's back in frustration before turning away. Calling his friends over, he quickly explained that there was another place to search for Hobs, and that they were to come with him. Without checking if they were following Roland headed east. The pace he set forced them to run in order to keep up. There would be trouble if Ren found Hobs before Roland did.

Pol made the pretense of a continued search for a bit longer before calling a halt for the night. It was too dark to continue, and if they were to continue this meaningless searching, it would be best to do so in the morning. For now they would return to town while they could still see clearly.

Roland and his friends were familiar with the terrain surrounding the river; this meant they were able to move swiftly. It wasn't until the terrain started rising and the ground became uneven that they slowed their pace. It would be ironic if he broke his neck while tracking Hobs, Roland thought caustically.

"Ease up, Rol." Cades' weariness was evident in his voice as he struggled for breath. "What's so important anyway?"

"You thick or what? We need to find Hobs before Ren does."

"Why does it matter so much anyway?" Piers chimed in. He was tired and wanted to head home and eat.

"You two saw the bruises we made this morning—you think Ren is gonna just ignore them?"

"You fight with Hobs all the time. What's different this time?"

Piers wasn't going to let this go, Roland thought. "The difference is, my pa told me to stop fighting and I didn't. Not only did I *NOT* stop but we beat him pretty good—*THAT* is gonna be trouble. Now shut up and move."

They slowed as they reached the edge of the forest. Roland paused while looking around to examine the forest. The trees here weren't as close together as they were near Redwood. They were skirting the northern edge, darting between the trees that dotted the hills in the area. Ahead, growing with every step was Deadmans Knoll.

A distant flash of light from the knoll arrested their progress. Within seconds a concussive sound washed over them which they had never heard before then earth moved under their feet. As quickly as it had begun it was over leaving the faltering daylight that much darker.

Something was happening, and not knowing what it was grew into a nagging fear that ate away at Roland's mind. Was Hobs the cause of what had just happened?

Piers grabbed Roland's shoulder. "There, moving in the brush," he hissed softly.

Roland followed his extended arm as he pointed to the southeast. What he saw drew a quick reaction forcing him to drop to ground, dragging his friends down with him.

"Shutter those lanterns now."

As he watched in the direction Piers had indicated, he could make out a light moving through the brush. He could just make out the form carrying the light. It was Ren heading toward Deadmans Knoll.

"Damn," Roland cursed softly. Ren was moving fast. What more had Lena told Ren? How much of what had been said between him and Hobs had she overheard? How much of the beating had she actually witnessed?

"Not good, not good at all."

"Isn't that Ren," Piers asked, quick with his identification.

"Of course it's Ren," Roland replied testily. "Keep the lights shuttered and let's follow him."

Things were going from bad to worse as far as Roland could tell. If his father found out about what they had done that morning—Roland cut that train of thought off fast. His father wouldn't find out if he could help it.

Roland stealthily altered his course to follow Ren, keeping to the shadows and using the brush for cover.

As he moved in the faltering daylight, Ren had a growing sense of being followed yet every time he glanced behind him he couldn't see anyone or anything and so he pressed on. He had to find Hobs—even then he feared he might be too late.

The real work started when he arrived at Deadmans Knoll. As he quartered the ground it wasn't long before he found something, not what he wanted but a clue at the least. Spotting something in the grass at the edge of a clearing he cautiously walked over to it—bending, he carefully picked up Hobs' bag. It was all the evidence he need to confirm that Hobs had been there, but where was he now?

Circling around the trampled grass, he found tracks leading around the northeast side of the main hill. Examining the grazer tracks, Ren quickly concluded that a few beasts had left the pack to return shortly after. He was also able to determine that Hobs had followed the tracks away from the herd, but he was unable to discover any signs of his return.

Hefting the comforting weight of the club in his hand, Ren followed the tracks. What he found when he rounded the bend stopped him dead in his tracks. Next to a large hole in the ground was the body of a large howler. The ground around the carcass showed signs of a struggle. As he moved forward carefully, his senses were assaulted by a strange odor that he couldn't identify. It grew stronger as he approached the edge of the pit. Smoke rose from the hole in curling wisps that rapidly dissipated in the wind that blew through the hills.

At the edge of the pit he found Hob's staff. Full of dread at what he might find he leaned over the edge and shone his light down, seeking any sign of Hobs within the depths. The drop was substantial he noticed – the light from his lamp barely illuminating the bottom of the hole. Ren exhaled the breath he had been holding without realizing it—no sign of Hobs.

A sound behind him brought him instantly to his feet, swiftly turning to confront the source of the sound. Dropping his bag, he brought his club up to the ready, his surprise turning swiftly to anger.

Roland quickly held his hands up as if to ward away Ren's club. He watched as Ren slowly lowered it back to his side.

"What are you doing here?" Ren questioned him harshly.

Roland paused briefly before answering—what had Ren found, if anything?

"When you didn't arrive at the river, my father grew worried. He sent us to find you."

Roland slowly approached Ren and peered down into the hole, Ren following his every move as Roland un-shuttered his lantern. Alarms sounded in Ren's head. Why had Roland's lantern been shuttered? Was he what he had sensed following him? Why the secrecy? What was he hiding?

Ren turned to face Roland fully.

"Roland I want some honesty from you. What did you do this morning?"

Roland looked full into Ren's face before replying. "Me? I didn't do anything at all. Why?"

"That's not what I heard Roland."

LENA. The bitch had to have seen the entire argument! Anger surged inside him and feeling his cheeks flush, Roland quickly turned away.

Ren's hand caught his shoulder and forcibly turned Roland back to face him. Roland reacted, shoving Ren. "Get your hands off me."

In horror, Roland watched as Ren faltered at the edge of the pit before he fell, screaming. Ren's body hit the bottom of the pit with a dull thud.

Roland rushed to the edge of the hole and looked down. His friends quickly joined him.

"What did you do?" Piers asked tentatively.

"Nothing—he grabbed me. I pushed him away so he would let go. Next thing I know he was falling."

"Man, I've never heard anyone scream like that. Do you think he's dead?" Cades asked.

Looking down, they could see the body. Ren wasn't moving at all.

"Well, I guess we need to climb down and check if he's alive," Roland told his friends sarcastically. "Who's going down?" Blank stares greeted his question. "Worthless lot you are. Guess I have to do all the work here."

Searching Ren's bag Piers found rope and with Cades' assistance they used it to carefully lower Roland into the pit. A quick check determined that Ren was dead. The headfirst fall had snapped his neck, killing him instantly. Roland quickly covered the body with rocks—that would have to suffice as a proper burial. He would have to inform the remaining council members of the accident.

"Pull me out, guys."

"Is he..." Piers started nervously once they had pulled Roland up, "dead?"

"Of course he's dead you dimwit," Roland replied sharper than he intended. "You saw him fall."

Both Piers and Cades regarded him for a second in muted silence.

"Cades grab Ren's gear. Piers take that stuff," Roland commanded pointing to Hobs' gear that Ren had found. "I need to talk to my pa about what happened here and he needs to know that there are howlers around.

Cades and Piers looked at the body of the howler before jumping to carry out his commands. Once everything was collected they headed back to town to report what had happened.

Chapter 5

An insistent banging on the door brought Jonaton awake from his much-needed sleep. It seemed as if he had just drifted off, only to be so rudely deprived of his rest.

Slipping into the warm robe that lay over the chair by his bedside, he slowly rose. The pain in his joints shot through his body as he stood. The joint pain was recent occurrence and Jonaton simply attributed it to growing old. All the same it reinforced the urgency that it was time that he started training a suitable replacement for his council seat. As far as the next leader of the council went, Ren would be a good choice once he stepped down. As such, Ren would need a strong ally to counter Pol's influence.

Pol could be volatile at times. You never knew what direction his arguments would go, or what measures he would oppose. Recently, he had successfully won his bid for Roland to become a council member when he retired. Jonaton felt this would be a disaster, even now. He and Ren had given in to Pol, unfortunately, on that matter since he was obstructing their proposal – the result was a disaster waiting to happen.

The banging on the door became more insistent, forcing Jonaton to hurry to answer it. Pain knifed through his joints as each step jarred them.

After unbolting the locking mechanism, he slowly opened the door. Outside he found Pol, Roland, and his two friends waiting for him quite agitated about something.

"Roland found Hobs' belongings but no sign of the boy," Pol stated before handing Jonaton the bag and staff that had been recovered.

Jonaton took a moment to examine Hobs' things briefly before setting them down.

"There has also been a tragic accident. Ren is dead."

"What!" Jonaton exclaimed in disbelief. He staggered back to sit as a strange pain shot down his right arm. "What happened to Ren?"

Jonaton turned to Roland as he answered, "We were searching for Hobs along the river but noticed that Ren wasn't with us. Naturally, my father was concerned so he sent us out to look for him." Roland indicated Piers and Cades.

"We were searching east when we found fresh grazer tracks. This made us think that perhaps Hobs didn't go to the river this morning and that he had gone somewhere else instead. As we searched the ground we discovered signs that indicated that Ren had found the same tracks and was following them.

"The path we followed led to Deadmans Knoll. When we got there, we found Ren at the edge of a pit holding Hobs' staff in his hand. I moved over to see if he required any help, but he grabbed me. I reacted by shoving him away in order to make him let me go." Roland paused. He appeared to be collecting himself in order to go on. "I didn't mean to, but he surprised me."

"What happened, boy?" Jonaton asked with growing fear…

"Ren stumbled on the edge of the pit—I watched him fall in. I tried to grab him, to do anything to prevent his fall, but I couldn't stop it."

Jonaton glanced at Piers and Cades. "Is this what happened?"

Neither spoke, but simply nodded their assent.

"Did anyone climb down and check Ren?" Jonaton asked, looking at Roland.

Roland nodded. "Yes sir, Piers and Cades lowered me down. It was obvious that his neck had broken from the fall. Rather than move him we built a pyre of rocks over his body to cover him."

Something didn't seem quite right here. "And what of Hobs' body?"

Jonaton saw the brief pause and questioning glance Roland sent to his father.

"Well?"

Roland continued, "No sir, we didn't find Hobs' body. But he must be dead also," he concluded swiftly.

"Why?" Jonaton replied with a piercing gaze at Roland, waiting for him to continue. After a substantial pause he turned to Pol, "We must continue the search for Hobs."

"No, Jonaton," Pol interrupted, "there are far more pressing matters to deal with than one worthless son of Redwood. Good riddance I say!" Pol's harsh words shocked Jonaton. "There was the body of a howler found in the same spot. I will not return to that spot if there are howlers preying in the area, and neither should anyone else."

Jonaton's face paled at the mention of the howler. He remembered well the last howler pack they had tracked and killed. He remembered the many lives that had been lost in that hunt.

"We also need to appoint a successor for Ren," Pol continued, interrupting Jonaton's thoughts.

"Who do you have in mind?" Jonaton asked sarcastically. "Roland?"

"Why not?" was Pol's quick reply, "I have been training him for this duty since he was a boy."

"Pol, you know my feelings on this matter. He will not sit on the same council as you. My answer is NO!" Jonaton replied with finality.

Roland was clearly taken aback by the vehemence of Jonaton's reply, and Pol appeared ready to fight.

"We will convene a council meeting tomorrow in order to discuss succession and the likely candidates," Jonaton concluded.

"Until then old man," Pol snapped before turning and stalking into the night, Roland and his cronies running quickly to catch up.

Jonaton slowly closed the door against the night, against the specter of disaster that had raised its ugly head. *"How could this have happened?"* he thought. *"Ren gone. Why?"* was all he could ask himself as he moved back to his bed where he sat considering the day's events and the vacant seat on the council – no matter whom he selected, Pol would vote no. Jonaton knew that no matter whom Pol selected, that person would likely not meet Jonaton's approval either. They would be locked into a stalemate unless he could find a way to sway the odds in his favor.

The normal selection process was for each council member to select a successor, one that the council would agree upon. The council member would then groom that person as his future replacement. This appointee would usually have years to learn the way the council operated before actually taking his position when his sponsor retired from service.

Roland was Pol's successor as the result of subtle manipulation. He had only gained approval because of his concessions in regards to the irrigation project Ren had sponsored. It was a project that benefited the community as a whole; yet Pol had repeatedly cast obstacles into the deliberations until Ren in frustration had agreed to Roland as Pol's successor. Only then did Pol agree to the project and remove all his objections.

Jonaton firmly believed that Pol had wanted the project also, but he had seized the opportunity to push Roland as his choice of successor. The ploy succeeded, and now Jonaton was left with the result. However, Roland would replace Pol—not Ren.

Never had they had a situation where a council member died without a successor, and he was unaware of any precedent to work from. If Hobs were here, they would take him into council since he had been formally adopted by Ren, and was being raised as his replacement. Pol would object, but at least there was a precedent to follow if that were an option. But it wasn't! Hobs was still missing, or even worse—dead.

Jonaton still wasn't sure why Ren had never told the boy that he had formalized the adoption. The papers had all been completed and sealed. *Ren must have had his reasons,* Jonaton thought as he climbed under the covers of his bed. This could be resolved in the morning, he thought to himself as he settled back down to sleep.

Sleep, however, eluded Jonaton for quite some time as he pondered the day's events. Who could replace Ren? After what seemed like hours of tossing and turning, a sly smile slowly spread on Jonaton's face. He knew how to proceed and it would work out well.

With the matter firmly in hand, Jonaton faded off to sleep.

Chapter 6

Archon was running diagnostics on the waste management systems when he received notification that the spinal implant was finished. He had long since compiled routines to handle all the mundane tasks that had to be completed, but he still liked to process some of them from time to time. It was these tasks kept him occupied during the long hours of silence. Gone were the days when his corridors had teemed with life, before the fall of Valara. He remembered well the day, so many long years ago when he had sent the final survivors out to integrate with the survivors of the genocide. Now all he had were dark, empty corridors haunted by specters of the past.

That was about to change!

Archon shunted the diagnostics off to a subroutine and examined the finished product. Rotating the implant slowly, he viewed it from every angle. Next, he reviewed the results of the diagnostics that had been run on it.

Everything checked out.

Satisfied that the implant would do exactly as intended, he initiated the final sequence. The implant, unlike the neural filaments, had a small power cell that would power the memory chip and mega-processor that Archon had added to the design. The mega-processor was a super computer that would process the body's neural functions. The power cell would be capable of powering the computer and neural net for much longer than the boy was likely to live.

It was a work of perfection Archon concluded.

Signaling a waiting android, he instructed it to transfer the implant to the medical bay. He tracked the android's progress with one part of his essence while initiating the next series of procedures in the medical bay.

Whirring into action, the medical unit reversed the position of the boy exposing his back so the laser scalpels could be brought to bear. With precise movements the lasers opened his back, exposing the full length of the spine.

Processing for a nanosecond, Archon considered the medical knowledge the Valaran had amassed—even with all their medical advancements, the Valaran had issues successfully repairing a severed spinal cord, and these successes had only come when the procedure was attempted on a Valaran. They had been able to use the neural filaments to give limited body functions back to the injured, but nothing of the magnitude Archon was attempting.

What Archon was attempting was revolutionary, and if it succeeded this boy would regain full use of his body! He was confident that it would work—*it had to!*

The medical unit continued running the program that had been initiated. With great care, the unit "split" the vertebrae, exposing the fragile spinal cord within and then positioned the spinal implant into place. It was the exact length of the boy's spinal cord, and as thin as the strings the Valaran musicians used on their instruments – it was a wonder of nano and neural technology combined.

As soon as it touched the spinal cord the nanobots commenced their work of integration. Archon monitored the progress as the implant and the spinal cord became, for all intents and purposes, ONE. With growing satisfaction, Archon noted that the implant appeared to be bridging the damaged spinal as the nanobots worked.

He would know if he was successful soon enough.

The neural filaments that had permeated the body extended their tendrils, integrating into the repaired spinal cord.

One final sequence remained—to connect a nano-port to the implant. Archon watched as the medical unit completed this crucial step. This port would be all but invisible to the human eye—its purpose was to grant access to upload and download information to the computer contained within the implant; and by extension—into the brain itself.

Once completed, the medical unit carefully repaired each vertebra, fusing them together. Completed, the unit applied a chemical agent to the boy's spine. This agent was similar to the one that had been used to strengthen and harden his bones; the difference, however, was that Archon added an additional chemical agent in order to retain the required flexibility in the disks.

With precision unmatched by any human, the medical unit closed the incisions and the procedure was done.

As he evaluated the results, Archon was pleased by what he read. Now for the real test...

With a single command Archon inserted a probe into the nano-port and initiated a diagnostic routine. He watched the results scroll by with mounting satisfaction; the neural network extended throughout his body, the control unit in the implant was online. The nanobots had attached themselves to the implant where they would remain dormant until such time as they were needed to repair any damage the body sustained.

Archon concluded that the final results exceeded all he had hoped for—one hundred percent success!

Now to test muscular responses; he initiated a program which would test his reflexes – starting with the feet Archon sent impulses that would move toes, feet, ankles, and knees first. He continued working various muscles until he finished with the opening and closing of the eyes. Through his link to the neural net, he could see what the eyes saw and hear what the ears heard. He even had access to the boy's memories.

When the diagnostic completed, Archon decided he would try one more thing—implanting memories directly to the brain and then retrieving those memories. This would be crucial to what he had planned.

Without questioning whether what he was doing was right or wrong, Archon uploaded a basic hand-to-hand combat training program. If the upload was successful then these new skills would be part of the boy's memory and the neural net would handle the impulses required for the muscles to perform the actions—the actions would be clumsy at the start but with practice they would become fluid.

Archon waited a few minutes until the *upload complete* response flashed. He initiated the retrieval of the program. Stroke for stroke Archon was able to recall the combat exercises from the brain. As he watched, the hands and arms mimicked the movements in accurate detail.

Archon was content. The only question remaining was *would the boy be able to retrieve and utilize the information?*

It was one thing for Archon to be able to do so while *jacked* into him; the real test would be how the boy would be able to perform.

Everything was set for the final phase so there was no point delaying the inevitable – he needed the full cooperation of the boy for his plan to work. Archon issued the final commands for the medical unit to wake him.

It felt as though he was rising from the depths of a river—every breath was a struggle as he grasped for air. No matter which way he turned, he couldn't break free. With a growing sense of panic, Hobs fought to regain consciousness. Strange smells assaulted his senses, forcing him to try unsuccessfully to open his eyes.

The smells were unlike any he had ever experienced, yet they were simple—the normal odors of the medical unit, something Hobs had never encountered before.

The next thing he was aware of was an unusual hum that he couldn't place. Having never been near mechanical equipment before, Hobs couldn't place the sounds. Everything he had ever imagined could not compare to what would assault his senses when he finally opened his eyes.

"I know you are awake, young human," Hobs heard a strangely hollow voice say. "Please acknowledge."

As Hobs opened his eyes he knew he should feel fear due to the strange surroundings, but instead he felt calm and alert. He was unaware that Archon had initiated a calming response using the neural interface still connected to the back of his neck. Reactions that would have been normal in this situation were quietly suppressed.

"I am Archon," the voice continued. "I run the facility in which you find yourself. Can you sit up?"

"I think so." Feeling a bit stiff, Hobs put words into action and sat up.

He tried to recall how he had gotten here. He thought carefully yet try as he might he couldn't recall what had happened. The last thing he could recall was taking the grazers to pasture in the morning, then NOTHING.

"Where am I? What happened to me?"

"You are not ready for that information yet, young human..." the voice continued, but this time it was in his head.

Is this a dream? Hobs thought confused. If so it was unlike any dream he had ever had; everything around him was so vivid and odd.

Hobs felt a slight pinch at his neck as Archon retracted the uplink from the nano-port. "OUCH!"

"Apologies, young human," Archon began, but Hobs interrupted.

"HOBS!" he screamed in frustration. "My name is Hobs Noller! Not young human."

Memories of what happened flooded into Hobs' brain—the howlers, the fight, and then he had fallen. *I died, didn't I?* Then the flashing light...

Archon continued, "Hobs..." he paused briefly to allow Hobs a moment to gather himself. "You were severely injured in a fall and inadvertently discovered my facility. Due to my programming I could not let you die though it may have been better for the safety of this facility if I had. Radical surgery was performed on you in order to restore full bodily function."

"Surgery?" The voice was using words that were strange and unknown to Hobs. He had no idea what was going on and panic was rising within him. "I want to go home!"

"Apologies for the unfamiliar words. It would not be safe for you to go home yet, I'm sorry – for now I have prepared food and a place where you can rest. Please follow unit X21 to your quarters. Anything you require will be provided.

"Why are you keeping me here?"

"As I said, it would not be safe for you to leave yet. You need time to rest and recover. Also, there is a request I would like to make of you but it can wait until you have recovered from your trauma and we have had time to talk."

The door opened with a *whoosh* causing Hobs to spin around. He grasped the edge of the bed as a wave of nausea swept through his body.

"I think you may be right about me needing some rest." Hobs regarded the strange metal man that had entered the room before asking, "Are you X21?"

No response! The promise of food however elicited a reaction in Hobs. He realized that he was hungry, so he would eat and then figure a way to get out from this place.

"Apologies again, young Hobs," he heard the disembodied voice say. "My androids do not have the facilities for speech, simply follow X21 where he leads you."

More strange words, Hobs thought.

"Thank you…Archon."

Rising from the medical bed, he approached what could only be an X21. The android turned and led the way from the medical facility. Archon issued commands to X21 to lead Hobs to the training barracks. There he would have a room with food, an access terminal, and the use of the training center with any fitness equipment he could need. He issued orders for a hot meal and beverage to be waiting for Hobs. A mild sedative was added to the drink; Hobs would need real sleep now in order to finish the healing process.

He watched as Hobs followed the android through the facility, his eyes looking around in wonder as he examined the smooth walls and the doors with strange words and their secrets hidden within. The android didn't allow time for Hobs to explore as it led him deeper into the base.

Archon saw Hobs enter the room he had prepared and look around. Hobs noted the clothes that were laid out on the bed and promptly put them on. While they were a bit utilitarian the fit was good.

Next, as anticipated, the smell of the hot meal caught Hobs' attention. Moving to the food dispenser, he sampled what was there. With obvious hunger, Hobs finished the meal swiftly and drank the beverage.

The effects of the sedative were fast; Hobs moved to the bed and fell asleep as soon as his head hit the pillow.

Archon shifted his attention back to the interrupted diagnostics that the subroutine had been running.

Chapter 7

It was early when Jonaton rose and began his preparations for the day. An unusual aching in his head prevented him from sleeping any longer. These headaches had been occurring more often lately, and they were beginning to trouble him. He had cut back on his obligations some, thinking he had been working too hard, but it hadn't helped.

He had been serving Redwood for over forty years. During that time he had many good memories—his fondest ones as the senior council member were presiding over the equinox festivals with the union ceremony. The union was a five-year commitment to each other; at the end of five years the couple could either enter into a permanent union, or go their separate way. Any children born of the union would be cared for by the mother and supported by the father. Jonaton was pleased that more often than not the couples choose to remain together.

Many couples had taken their vows with him over the years during the festivals. There was always at least one couple that participated in the special occasion marked by couples taking their vows of union and then having them sealed before those attending by the ritual of anointing. During the ritual, each townsperson would pour a bit of the blood red Graz wine over the couple's heads to signify love, happiness, and long life. To end the ceremony the couple would drain the remaining Graz wine from the cup to symbolize the completion of the union.

Jonaton's thoughts wandered back to the first equinox he had presided over as senior council member. There had been two unions that year. Pol and Atina had been one, and the other had been Ren and Elena. Elena, his lovely daughter! He had been such a proud father that day. Jonaton remembered his joy that Elena had found someone special with whom to enter the union.

Frowning, he remembered that even on that day Pol had been at odds with Ren. He wasn't happy having to share his union day with them. In spite of the hostility, Ren never seemed to notice. He was fully occupied with his Elena.

Two years later Fre was born. Never had there been a happier grandfather! Jonaton adored the boy almost as much as his father and mother did. He was such a tiny baby, Jonaton thought as he recalled the times he had held him in his arms. There had been such high hopes for Fre's future.

He was thrilled when Ren and Elena decided to finalize their union after the initial five-year commitment—they were good for one another.

When Fre reached the age of four, Jonaton commenced with Fre's education. He was determined that Fre would be his replacement on the council since he had no sons of his own. His wife having passed the year prior meant there would be no chance of any either.

Fre was a fast learner, and within a year he was reading the simple books designed for children. It was puzzling to Jonaton why more parents didn't want their children to learn how to read. He felt reading and numbers were necessary skills required by anyone in order to succeed. Many didn't see the need of a proper education unfortunately, being content to learn their trade from their mothers and fathers, and that was enough for them.

They had no hope or goals for the future. They felt no need to improve themselves or their community. Oh, they would rise and help with the projects the council set forth, but planning and being creative on their own just didn't happen.

Fre was different.

He would have made a perfect council historian, taking over that mantle from Jonaton when he chose to retire. But it was not to be!

The child had died twelve years ago during the plague that had ravished the town. The same plague had taken his Elena and both of Hobs' parents. He remembered how devastated Ren had been by his losses.

Jonaton's thoughts turned to Hobs and his parents. His brow furrowed as he remembered them. They were a peculiar pair. They weren't from Redwood, and he had never been able to determine where they had come from. The nearest town was two days' journey to the south, and it was rare to ever see anyone from there. They both had the same jet-black hair that Hobs had inherited, and the same strange eyes.

Rowena, Hobs' mother, was pregnant with him when they arrived. Being outsiders, many people shunned them—not wanting Rowena and Parem to settle in Redwood. Jonaton, however, had stepped in and persuaded the council to accept them. The town should never turn anyone away, he argued; new blood was always good for the town. Once he had gained acceptance for them to settle, he organized the community to help build their home. Until its completion Jonaton allowed the couple to live with him.

Two months after their home was completed, Rowena delivered a baby boy, whom she named Hobs Noller. Parem integrated his family into Redwood's community with ease. He was always willing to help others and proved to be a wealth of useful knowledge.

He remembered the assistance Parem had provided to Ren and his father, improving the refining processes they used in the smithy. The results were purer metals that they were then able to fashion easier. He also showed them how certain metals could be mixed to form stronger alloys.

Parem had drawn designs for new farming implements that could be crafted with the new metal. Ren had been excited; he had obtained his father's permission and had worked on the new designs day and night. When done, the farming tools were given to the farmers to test—the new tools allowed the farmers to work the fields with improved efficiency. Their new plows lasted much longer than their old ones had, not breaking as often, so they were able to plow the fallow ground much faster.

The friendship between Ren and Parem had blossomed as a result. Jonaton knew that there were a number of other things Parem had done for Ren – he had taught him to read better than he had been able to prior; he had also taught him to do his numbers. Jonaton suspected that if he had lived longer, then he might have been able to help Ren reach the point where he would have been able to replace Jonaton as historian.

That was all before the plague!

Twelve tragic years ago!

Jonaton could still remember the wails of grief from the survivors over those who were lost to them. Parem and Rowena had worked relentlessly during that plague. Their knowledge of the various herbs that could heal was second to none. The town healer had been grateful for all the assistance they provided as well as for the knowledge they brought.

Their medicines helped many make it through that terrible time. Their insistence on isolation of the victims turned the tide in controlling the disaster. Unfortunately it proved bitter for Jonaton and Ren when Elena and Fre both contracted the plague. They were isolated and the loss of contact with them had been as if someone had taken a knife and cut out their hearts. They could only wait and hope while Elena and Fre battled the disease.

Jonaton was crushed when the news came that Fre had died. It had taken all his strength not to break down while comforting his grief-stricken son by union and then Elena died shortly after. Jonaton felt that she had given up her will to fight when Fre died and simply slipped away.

Many others died that year, but the greatest loss to the town was Rowena and Parem. In spite of all the precautions taken, they contracted the disease – with their resistances already severely lowered due to their efforts, they quickly succumbed to it.

Ironically, they were the last deaths from the plague that had decimated the village.

During his time of grieving Ren constructed the monument that stands in the center of town as a remembrance of his friends and family. Then he took the orphaned Hobs as his son and raised him. He had confided that it was the least he could do for his lost friend. Jonaton completed the documents of adoption five years later at Ren's request.

Now Ren was gone and Hobs was missing. Would the tragedies in his life never end?

The decision that faced Jonaton now was the need for a new council member—one who was able to take on the tasks of historian. It wasn't an option! The records had to be kept. Jonaton had diligently preformed this task for the last twenty-five years and knew that it was time for the responsibility to be passed on.

He knew whom he would choose—that had been determined last night before he fell asleep. He simply needed to confirm what he already knew – he needed the precedent for what he was about to propose and that would be found in the records. He had even worked through how to get his selection accepted.

Jonaton locked his house and proceeded to the council building. It was a simple building with two rooms: one for meetings and the other for the Hall of Records. The Hall of Records was built into a cave in the rock face the building was built against.

He paused at the simple black memorial standing in front of the Council building. On it was inscribed a list of the names of those who had died during the plague. The names of Parem and Rowena topped the list in honor of their self-sacrifice in helping others.

He wept softly as his finger traced the names of Fre and Elena. The loss weighed heavily on his heart even now, twelve years later. He paused, taking a minute to regain his composure before entering the building. *Enough of the past*, he thought to himself, it was time to guarantee the future.

Once inside he proceeded to the Hall of Records without a pause. Unlocking the door, he entered and lit the lamps in the room. Selecting the volume he required he moved to the table in the middle of the room. Reverently he turned the pages of the book—finding the list of those he had taught over the years. Those whose parents weren't afraid of knowledge! After checking the list, he confirmed that there was only one name that stood out above the rest. Only one with the reading and writing skills required of the person who would be the historian—Abigail!

Pol wouldn't like this choice. It had been many long years since a woman had sat on the council, but the precedent was there. Closing the book with care, he gathered a few items that he would require— then carefully locking the Hall of Records he went back outside where he began ringing the bell of assembly.

Pol was just finishing breaking his fast when he heard the bell. *"What is that old man up to?"* he thought.

"Roland," he yelled for his son, "get dressed now! This is an important day for you. We must get to the council hall quick."

Without waiting to see if Roland heard him he hurried to the hall. People were already starting to fill the building.

"Make way!" With a sharp bark of command the townsfolk fell aside, opening a path for Pol. He took his place at the table in the center of the room where Jonaton was already seated. The smile on Jonaton's face caused Pol to pause in surprise. *What is the old man up to?* Pol thought to himself grimly, regardless of what it was he had a few surprises ready for Jonaton. Before this day was over, Roland would be on the council.

"Order," Jonaton commanded once Pol had seated himself.

The crowd quieted themselves as Jonaton slowly rose to address them. He looked around the room before starting. "Friends," Jonaton began, pausing briefly to collect himself, "today we meet in the midst of great tragedy. As many of you already know, yesterday we lost Ren to an unfortunate accident. To compound this tragic event, I have to report that Hobs is still missing. After this meeting, we will discuss continuing our search for Hobs – not along the river, however, but at Deadmans Knoll. Added to this is the threat of howlers as reported by Pol and Roland. We will take the necessary steps to hunt them down while we conduct our search."

Jonaton calmed the rising murmurs of the assembly at the mention of the howlers. "There is nothing to fear; we have dealt with howlers before. However, first we have a great task before us. We must select a new council member."

Jonaton saw the triumphant grin that lit Pol's face and he paused before continuing. Now was the time to take the air out of Pol once and for all.

"In addition, this council member will be trained to take over my responsibilities as the Council Historian," he concluded.

The impact of Jonaton's statement hit Pol like a rockslide. The old man had outwitted him; there was no way Roland could be Historian. Pol scowled at Jonaton's back but Jonaton wasn't finished.

"My esteemed colleague," Jonaton continued, gesturing to Pol, "has repeatedly asked for his son Roland to be considered, so let's consider him. Roland, come forward!" He spoke with command.

Pol watched as Roland walked forward to the table and presented himself to the assembled. Maybe, just maybe, there was still hope.

What hope there might have been was dashed when Jonaton picked up the book, parchment, and pen that had lain out of view on Ren's seat. He watched as Jonaton opened the book and commanded Roland to start reading.

Pol had tried to teach Roland to read but the boy wasn't very good at it. He listened as his son stumbled over the words before hanging his head in shame.

"Enough Roland, thank you." Jonaton said, handing the boy the parchment and pen. "Record the purpose of this meeting please."

Roland took the pen and parchment and just stood there. After a few minutes he placed them on the table in front of him. Bowing his head he simply said, "I can't, sir."

"Then you are not fit for the position. Return to your place," Jonaton concluded.

Pol could only watch the humiliation of his son in silence, thinking about how he would get even with the old man. He resolved that this would be the last time he or his son would be humiliated like this in front of the community.

Jonaton turned to the assembled. He looked on the faces of his friends and neighbors as they turned to him with expectation. They were the faces of those with whom he had lived and worked for years. These were people who looked to him for direction, for leadership— they looked to him to make the right choices. He was not going to let them down. He was about to make a radical decision, but one that was in the best interests of the community. Would they accept his decision without question? Would they be willing to go down the path he was about to set before them?

"Roland was the only name brought forth and as you can see he lacks the skills required for the seat in question. I do not want anyone in this room to think that this test was conducted in order to humiliate Roland. It was not! The council mandates require this simple test to validate a candidate's qualifications. I am sure he has the makings of a good councilman in the future, as a replacement for Pol when he retires. However," Jonaton paused to let his words sink in before continuing, "not as the council historian. Does anyone else have a nomination that they would like to present for consideration?"

Jonaton looked around the room expectantly. "No one? In that case there is a nomination that I would like to make. A candidate whom I feel has the requisite qualifications to perform the role in question. The person I am presenting for consideration is of upstanding character in the community, and above reproach."

He studied the faces as a touch of anxiety filled his mind. *What if they reject my choice?* He thought.

"I have spent a long, tumultuous night considering this decision before us. My morning was spent studying the records for precedent. What I was able to determine was that there were three people who could have filled the role. One was Ren; his unfortunate passing has eliminated him from consideration."

Jonaton paused to collect himself as tears threatened to overwhelm him. His friend and son-in-union was lost to him forever.

"The second was Hobs. Both Ren and I worked diligently on his education, and he would have been adequate to fulfill the position."

A gasp of disbelief from the assembly required Jonaton to pause. Everyone had thought of Hobs as a simple man, unworthy of such a lofty position. Jonaton knew better. Glancing at Roland, he noted the look of open hatred on his face before continuing.

"Therefore, there is only one person left who possesses the requisite skills to perform the tasks required of the historian—that is Abigail!"

Many things happened at once—Pol leaped to his feet shouting in defiance, and simultaneously the crowd burst into cheers and a few arguments.

"ORDER!" Jonaton shouted to be heard. "ORDER!"

It was minutes before the crowd quieted enough to allow Jonaton to continue. As he prepared to explain his reasoning, Pol spoke out quickly, interrupting him.

"You are out of line Jonaton. Women have never been on the council and I will not allow it to happen now. What makes you think we would accept your nomination?"

Jonaton's piercing eyes stared at Pol until he reluctantly sat down. The room became deathly silent as all eyes focused on Jonaton, waiting for his response.

"Actually, there is precedent as you will see. Abigail, come forward!"

Abigail slowly moved to the table, her slight frame visibly shaking. Afraid to look at anyone around her, she slowly brushed her light auburn hair from her face and wrapped her shawl tighter around her shoulders before focusing her eyes on Jonaton.

"Abigail," he said more gently, "I would like you to read the same passage which I just asked Roland to read."

Abigail looked at Jonaton for a moment longer before lowering her eyes to the book. She briefly examined the page he wanted her to read. With a growing sense of understanding of what he was doing she proceeded to read the passage.

"After a long and hard debate today the council voted unanimously on the appointment of Brenda to the council. All arguments regarding her gender were put aside as she was determined to be a suitable replacement for her father, Orin. Further, the council decided unanimously to bestow on her the title of Historian. As such, the keys to the Hall of Records were presented to her for safekeeping."

"That is enough," Jonaton interrupted the reading. "You have proven sufficiently that you can read the writings. Now," he continued as he handed Abigail a quill, "write what is occurring here today with as much clarity as you can, understanding that it is for future generations to read. Remember that what you write could potentially be used to validate decisions made by future councils."

Abigail paused, then bending over the parchment she started writing the events of the meeting. When she was done she put down the pen and looked up at Jonaton. The pride in his eyes, and the slight smile on his face told her everything she needed to know. She had done well!

She watched as Jonaton handed the parchment to Pol; he glanced at it in disgust before throwing it back on the table.

"My vote is still no!" he vehemently stated, his face a mask to the emotions boiling within him.

"As I knew it would be," Jonaton replied, surprising Pol. "And since we are in deadlock, I am invoking a long unused right as council leader. It is written in the laws of assembly that in the event of deadlock, when deciding a position as vital as Historian, the leader of council can order a vote of the assembled." He paused. "All in favor say AYE!"

He surveyed the crowd as shouts of AYE filled the hall. "Those not in favor say NAY."

Pol was vocal in his NAY.

To Jonaton's delight, the few scattered NAYS in the crowd were not enough to turn the obvious result. "Motion passed! Abigail is our new Historian and third council member," he concluded triumphantly.

Then with great ceremony he bowed and gently kissed her hand in respect. Out of the corner of his eye, he observed Pol acknowledge her choice—his bow granting her the barest respect he could manage without insult.

Rising, Jonaton noted the flush on Abigail's checks. She was such a beautiful woman to have no man with whom to share her life—a widow, he contemplated quietly. Her husband had died in a tragic mining accident. His passing had left Abigail with a young daughter to raise on her own. Locating her daughter in the crowd, he could see the pride in her eyes for her mother. Abigail had done a wonderful job with the responsibility. He felt confident that the same care and nurturing she had demonstrated with her daughter would make her a competent councilwoman.

"My dear, I pass on to you the mantle and title of Historian. With the due honor and respect befitting the position and I present to you the keys to the Hall of Records."

With a properly respectful bow he handed the keys of office to her. Gently guiding her by the shoulder, he helped Abigail around the table to take the center seat. He turned to the assembled and announced with joy, "I present to you Abigail, Historian of Redwood, respected Councilwoman."

Then to the excitement of all he poured the vial of Graz wine on her head, anointing her to office.

Lena, standing in the crowd, beamed at her mother with all the pride and love only a daughter could have.

Chapter 8

Hobs woke from his sleep surprised that he was feeling refreshed and better than he had for a long time. When he opened his eyes, he realized that everything hadn't been a dream. His surroundings were as strange as they had been the day before. Where was he?

With an effort he pushed these thoughts from his mind; sitting up, he examined the room around him; it was a small room with smooth walls that were made of a substance Hobs could not identify, even the sheets and blanket had an unusual texture and feel to them. The bed extruded from the wall without any visible seam that he could find. There were three rectangles on the wall next to the bed that opened when he moved his hand over them. Inside he found clothing similar to those he had put on the night before; another wave of his hand closed the drawer. Two doors led from the room; one to a large open space, the other to a small cubicle – Hobs decided to leave the exploration of the cubicle for later. He turned back to the room where his attention was draw to a small table against the wall opposite of the bed; a peculiar device was perched on top of it; beside it was the alcove in which he found his food the night before.

A mechanical sound heralded the arrival of breakfast. He watched as the back of the alcove slide open and a tray of food was disgorged into the enclosure. The aroma from the food dispenser was enticing bringing along with it the realization that he was hungry again. He moved to the dispenser and took the food plate to the table and started eating.

Archon, he thought. Yes, that was the name. He must have left the food for him.

"Thank you for the food Archon."

There was no response yet Hobs knew he hadn't imagined Archon.

After finishing his food, he relieved himself in the small alcove that he had discovered earlier. His initial assessment of its purpose was correct—and such a marvel the cubicle was. He watched in wonder as he played with the silver handle that magically made the water disappear, only to reappear moments later. It was much better than the pots they used in Redwood. You had to constantly take them out to the pit in order to empty them. Plus this room smelled much nicer, he thought, chuckling to himself.

Hobs began to wonder where the disembodied voice was as he entered the quiet training facility. He stood just inside the entrance, looking around in awe as he surveyed the vast room. Nothing in the room was familiar but for some strange reason all the equipment *felt* as if it belonged. He moved onto mats that covered the floor in the center of the room. They were soft under his bare feet, but with a certainty he knew the function they served.

After careful consideration, he decided to test what he "remembered." He proceeded to move through a series of hand-to-hand combat drills. When completed, he reflected in wonder on what he had just done. He was extremely clumsy on his first attempt through, so as an experiment he tried the kata again. This time the motions, while still awkward, were more fluid; it was almost as if his body was getting use to them. As he contemplated what he was doing, he found that he could place names to each movement that he had executed.

One more time...

The first step was come to the ready position.

He followed that by turning left into a low front stance with his left foot forward, body low to the ground, this was followed with the execution of a downward block over the exposed leg.

Hobs paused, how could he know this?

He continued by shifting forward into another low front stance with his right foot forward, followed with the execution of a right punch.

Rapidly Hobs completed the remaining steps of the drill. With growing realization, he discovered that this was only the first of many drills that he could recall. He shifted into the next drill, followed by five more—since each new kata built on the ones before he was able to execute each new one faster than the prior. The moves become a bit less mechanical with each execution.

Hobs completed the final drill and stopped in disbelief. He had never done these moves before. How could he know them?

It was like a dance of motion and he was the star of the show. He continued to practice the various movements he "*remembered*" over the next two hours, perfecting the skills he "*knew*."

Archon watched as Hobs executed the drills – while he started awkwardly, the boy rapidly improved in his execution as *muscle memory* kicked in with the help of the implant. He was pleased with how well Hobs was handling the basic hand-to-hand program he had uploaded. He observed as Hobs' execution transformed from clumsy to catlike movement; he had a grace that gave him the potential of becoming a seasoned fighter, and his body was in exceptional shape in spite of the lifestyle and diet he was accustomed to eating. Archon was enriching the food he provided with the vitamins and minerals that Hobs was deficient in – this would help with the muscle development Hobs required.

Hobs had finished his workout and moved to the weight training part of the facility. Archon watched as Hobs considered the various pieces of equipment before selecting one to try. Since Hobs had never used one, his experimentation didn't succeed very well.

Time to intervene...

"Hobs," Archon said, surprising the young man. "Would you like to know how to use this equipment?"

"I'm not sure," was Hobs' confused reply. "I know things that I shouldn't, yet I have no memory of learning the things I just did but my body knows them... What's happened to me? How can I know things that I never learned?"

The confusion was clear in Hobs' voice, as well as the slight edge of panic and fear. Archon knew that this was a moment of potential crisis. This was the time for Hobs to make his decision—a decision that would impact the plan Archon had conceived, a decision that could alter Archon's fate forever!

"There was extensive damage to your body as the result of your fall. I repaired this damage, yet part of the repair required the introduction of advanced technology. It was a necessary measure if you were to regain the full use of your body – without this technology you would have remained paralyzed," Archon replied.

Hobs remembered stories of a boy who had once fallen and, as a result, couldn't move his legs. He had to be helped everywhere, including the privy. He was glad that fate didn't wait for him.

"Thank you Archon, for all you have done for me," Hobs said sincerely. "Yet your words are strange, and they don't explain how I can remember these things."

"I was getting to that young Hobs," Archon admonished like a teacher to his errant pupil. "Part of the 'tech' interfaces with your nervous system and brain…"

"STOP," Hobs yelled in exasperation, "I don't understand the words you're using. *This*," he waved his arms to encompass the facility around him, "is all confusing and new to me—isn't there any way you can explain it simpler?"

"I can provide you with the means to understand the explanation the same way you *learned* the hand-to-hand drills if you wish," Archon offered.

"I'm not sure how you did that, but I like what I now know, so YES I would like to know more," Hobs replied emphatically with the realization that he meant what he said. Having to defend himself over the years, he realized the value in what he now knew. He had no clue how he had "learned" his new knowledge, but he knew with a certainty that Archon held the answers to all the questions he had ever had. Maybe Archon would be able to answer some of the questions that gnawed at him. Maybe…

"Please move over to the data terminal by the wall," Archon directed.

Hobs looked over to the entrance and saw what must be the terminal Archon was referring to – it was similar to the device on the table in his room; he moved over to it and waited expectantly.

"For now we must use a link cable, but with your permission we will add a transmitter/receiver later," Archon began. "For now let us not question how we will do this."

The door opened, surprising Hobs. He calmed when it turned out to be another of the strange metal men with a thin cable in his hand. Hobs watched as the android plugged one end into the terminal and then turned to face Hobs while it patiently waited—for what? Hobs wasn't sure.

"Hobs, the cable must be attached to an access port that I placed in the back of your neck." Archon watched as the boy's hands moved to his neck.

It took a long moment but he was able to detect the small port that had been placed there. Archon was impressed when the boy simply turned his back to the android and lifted his hair so the uplink could be attached.

Archon had three programs selected for this upload. With satisfaction, he noted that he had anticipated this event correctly. Without hesitation he started the upload of the programs to Hobs.

The first program was biology and basic medical training. The second one was a course in technical fundamentals and terminology. The final program was one that Archon had added at the last moment. It contained a full weight-training program. Archon decided it would be expeditious to give Hobs training in a topic that he had demonstrated an interest in.

Transmission complete flashed the reply.

Memories that were both confused yet understood at the same time flooded Hobs' mind. He understood things that he hadn't before; words came unbidden to his mind, and he was surprised that he knew what they meant. How could this be? It was overwhelming...

The room started spinning around Hobs; with growing panic he sought to fight the nausea roiling in his stomach. Something wasn't right, Hobs thought as he collapsed unconscious to the floor.

For the first time in centuries, Archon felt panic. He ordered the android to carry Hobs back to his bed. Once there, he initiated various scans on Hobs. Everything checked out, so what was wrong?

Instructions were sent for the android to break a vial of smelling salts used to waken unconscious patients. As it passed the vial under Hobs' nose, his eyes flew open.

"Are you okay, Hobs?" Archon queried anxiously when the boy's eyes fluttered open.

"I feel..." Hobs paused for a moment to collect his thoughts before continuing. "Confused...fine. Actually, I feel more than fine—just overwhelmed. There is so much I don't know. Even with what you gave me I realize that there are so many things I still don't understand. There are terms I feel I should know but I can't quite place them; there are things I now know but I can't believe them – like that machine to work my abdominal muscles that I tried to use earlier—I know how it works now. It's..." He paused again. "It's amazing," he concluded with a hint of awe.

"You were telling me about the tech that you placed in my body. Can you finish your explanation now?" Hobs asked. "I believe I can understand it now."

"The trauma to your spine was severe. It had been damaged in the fall, leaving you paralyzed. You also had multiple breaks and fractures. Do you understand so far?"

Hobs nodded his assent, knowing but still not quite believing how he could.

"We placed neural filaments in your body after repairing the bones," Archon continued, while Hobs recalled what a neural filament was from his newly acquired memories. "These filaments integrated with your nervous system, giving you a second means of transmitting impulses and commands through your body. This wasn't enough to completely fix the trauma to your spine so I had an implant specially created to repair the spine. Once this was added, it 'bridged' the damage, giving you back your full range of motion. The neural filaments were then able to complete the integration in your body by connecting to the spinal implant."

Archon paused briefly. He knew this was the tact to take. He had monitored the emotional responses as Hobs had processed the new information. Knowledge would be the key to win Hobs' trust and confidence, and knowledge would be the weapon he would use.

"For reasons I will explain later, I added the uplink port that we just used rather than placing an uplink transmitter/receiver. This link is used to 'give' memories; this data is stored directly in your brain.

Humans only use a small portion of the brain as it is, and the information I uploaded was stored in the rarely used part. In the spinal implant there is a 'computer,'" Archon used the simple term so Hobs would understand. "That interfaces with your brain and allows you to access the full storage potential of your brain. You now have the capability of 'learning' a wealth of information never before possible by a human."

Archon instructed the android to hand Hobs the uplink cable.

"Keep this cable with you for now. It will allow you to upload information and programs as you wish from your terminal. Over time you will find that the more you access this knowledge you are learning, the easier it will become to recall. In other words, you will train your brain to automatically access these new storage areas through repetitive recall and use."

Hobs could almost hear a smug satisfaction in Archon's voice as he continued, "You have but to select what you want to learn."

Disbelief slowly turning to comprehension, Hobs replied, "I understand." To his surprise he did, limited though that knowledge still was.

The satellites in orbit above Cygnus Prime continued their programmed tasks day in and day out. Relays clicked, and signals were sent and received—processes that had continued for centuries. Over the past few days this routine had been altered.

An unusual phenomenon had been detected—an explosion. Programming required an intensive scan of the area of infraction when anomalies occurred. Today there was another anomalous discovery; an appropriate entry was made, noting unusual increases in power emanations coming from a small area of the planet below. Programming, not required since the satellite had been placed in orbit clicked into action resulting in a burst transmission—destination Scaria. That the transmission would take three days to reach its first relay in the journey was of no consequence to the machine.

With the message sent, the satellite shunted the information into storage and returned to its monitoring of the planet.

The moment the transmission was dispatched, Archon was aware of it. With a sinking realization, he knew that there was only a short amount of time left before the Scarian would arrive to investigate the planet. In an attempt to salvage what he could, he activated long dormant point defense systems. The order was given to terminate the ten Scarian satellites located around his planet.

Bunkers long hidden in order to conceal them from the satellites opened to reveal the laser cannons within. Bursts shot skyward, blotting the satellites from the sky one after another in brilliant explosions. Mission completed! The bunkers were closed and sealed once more. Androids were sent to cover any traces that they had ever existed.

The residents of Redwood and several other towns saw something shocking; it was something that they would not soon forget. Without understanding what it was, they watched as the lasers shot skyward on their mission of destruction. The day the lights danced in the sky would be a story they regaled their children and their children's children with for years to come.

What had caused these lights was something most would never learn, or comprehend even if they did discover the cause.

It was only a matter of time now. Hobs had to be ready soon or everything would be in vain and Hobs' life would be in danger!

Chapter 9

Abigail stood by the memorial in the plaza watching as the lasers struck skyward. Like the others in Redwood she had no clue what they meant, but with realization she knew that what she had witnessed was something significant and, as such, it was her duty to record these events.

She had spent the afternoon in the Hall of Records with Jonaton learning what her new duties entailed. It was a wonder to her that she had been selected for this honor. How proud Lena had been when they reached home after the council meeting.

Abigail smiled to herself as she recalled Lena's joy.

She was proud of her girl and the woman she was growing into. With her new responsibilities, Lena would have to take over Abigail's position at the day center for the town children. She would be able to teach them, just as Abigail had tried over the years—some with success, others not so much—*like Roland.*

With Lena she had succeeded. She could read and write quite well. With her loving support, she would continue to blossom. Abigail would see to it when it was time for her to step down from the council that Lena would replace her – that, however, would be years from now. For now she had to learn what was required.

With a final glance skyward, Abigail turned and entered the council hall. She had to record these events while they were fresh in her mind. Using the small key Jonaton had given her, she unlocked the Hall of Records and entered.

She grabbed the current journal from its pedestal and moved to sit quietly at the table where they had been working earlier. She had chronicled the events from earlier in the day already—now, somehow, she had to put into words the lights they had all seen dancing in the afternoon sky.

What caused them?

She was certain Pol would be quite vocal about his thoughts, saying something stupid about how Hobs and Ren were to blame for the lights. He would continue by insisting that they had disturbed something when they went to Deadmans Knoll.

She laughed at that thought, hearing him clearly in her mind.

There was, however, a single question that persisted—the one she mulled over and over in her mind—where was Hobs. He had not been found; maybe he did have something to do with them.

Pol's innuendo and accusations had stirred the town up so much that no one was willing to return to the Knoll: to search for Hobs, or to retrieve Ren's body so that he could be given a proper burial. Abigail regretted both deeply—Ren had always been so kind to her and Lena after Jason had died.

She had also observed how Lena watched Hobs when he wasn't looking. That bothered Abigail just a little. Hobs was different in ways that she couldn't understand; yet Rowena had been her friend and she was determined that she wouldn't stand in Lena's way if Hobs was her choice for a life mate—but there were better choices for her.

Then there was Roland! Something about Roland made Abigail shudder—he was the son of his father for sure. Abigail was glad that she had refused Pol years ago when he had attempted to court her. Everything Pol stood for revolted Abigail. She had watched as Pol constantly resisted project after project that could only help the town. All that was about to change.

She lived a happy life in Redwood and it was about to get better.

She returned to the task at hand and started writing about the lights that danced in the sky. The sooner done, the quicker she would get home to her Lena.

Fifteen minutes later, with a final stroke of her quill she finished.

DONE!

She placed the quill and ink back in the drawer, blowing gently on the page to help the ink dry. When satisfied that it was dry enough, she closed the journal and returned it to the pedestal where it would wait until the next event worth chronicling.

Looking around the room, Abigail realized that spending her days in this room would be a pleasure. What an opportunity she now had to read the years and years of history contained within the pages stored in this room. There was so much that she could learn and she relished the opportunity. History surrounded her here; she could almost feel it as a tangible presence as she cast her glance about the room.

The sound of shuffling feet brought her swiftly back to reality as she whirled around to face whoever was there...

She hid her dismay when she saw that it was Pol. "Can I help you?"

"No, but I can help you if you wish to succeed on the council," Pol replied.

"What do you mean?" she queried Pol.

"I can make your time on the council very pleasant," Pol stated. "Or not," he ended ominously.

"How many times do I have to tell you no Pol?" Abigail replied, stopping short when Pol started laughing.

"Oh how you continue to misunderstand me. You do me a great dishonor Abigail," Pol concluded with mock hurt.

Pol moved slowly into the room, glancing at the shelves filled with journals—he looked everywhere but at Abigail.

"I am thinking of an understanding between you and I, one that will see us both succeed," he continued, turning his gaze to Abigail. "I am speaking about Lena and Roland. Think of the alliance that their union could forge and the years it would last."

"If Lena agrees to Roland then it will be what it will be, but I will not force Roland on her even if it would make being on the council easier," Abigail replied forcefully.

"I hope you know what you are doing Abigail," Pol replied, turning to leave. "Jonaton won't live forever. I think his age is catching up with him already. Did you see how pale he looked in council this afternoon?"

With that ominous pronouncement Pol left the council building, leaving Abigail to consider what he had said regarding Jonaton. They were only words meant to scare her, of that she was certain, but she wouldn't take any chances. She would stop by and check on him before returning home for the evening.

Carefully locking the door to the Hall of Records, Abigail left the building and moved towards Jonaton's house. After she checked in on him she would have Lena take him some food for his evening meal.

Lena opened the door to her dark house. Her mother wasn't home, and with a smile breaking on her face, she was sure where she could be found. Her mother had to be at the council hall, going over the old records. She was proud of her mother. She worked hard and deserved the honor that Jonaton had conferred on her.

She didn't miss the look of humiliation on Roland's face as he left the building. The manner in which Jonaton had dealt with him was appropriate. Roland was a thug, nothing more, and Lena wanted nothing to do with him. He was constantly attempting to force his attentions on her even though she had made it abundantly clear she wasn't interested.

Since her mother wasn't home yet, Lena decided to start dinner. It had to be something special to celebrate the day's events. She thought about what she could make—they had some salted grazer meat left in the pantry—that would be a start, Lena thought. Some warm bread would be nice to go with the meat. Lena gathered the required ingredients. In no time she had the dough ready and covered so that it could rise properly for baking.

The next task was to prepare some vegetables for cooking; these she retrieved from the pantry. Vegetables in hand, she moved to the sink where she started washing them. She took care in peeling them—it wouldn't do for her mind to drift and end up cutting her hand by mistake.

But try as she might, her thoughts kept wandering. She couldn't get Hobs out of her mind, or the way Roland had treated him yesterday morning. Roland might have killed him if she hadn't stopped him. Now Hobs was missing and she was worried. What had happened to him? Would she ever see him again?

Hobs was her friend, and a very good one at that. She could tell him everything, her dreams, her fears, and even the simple things that happened day to day.

She knew her mother thought she was considering Hobs for union, but it wasn't that at all. Hobs understood her, and accepted her as she was. They had never spoken about or even considered entering the union with each other. They were friends, pure and simple. Besides, she had plans of her own regarding a union and was working toward it slow and steady, at her own pace. After all, it wouldn't do to scare her intended away before he knew he wanted her.

Roland, on the other hand, was obnoxious, annoying, rude, demanding—well, the list could go on, she thought. She didn't want anything to do with him. Yet he was spreading rumors in town that she was attached to him and that would have to stop. He would ruin all of her carefully laid plans.

With a slip of the knife Lena was brought back to the present. Pain shot through her hand; she observed with detachment as blood started oozing from where she had cut herself.

Drip...drip...drip, she heard as droplets of blood splashed onto the vegetables in the sink.

She opened the water spigot and carefully washed the cut; she knew it was important to make sure there was no contamination in the wound, and she had to determine how bad the cut was.

"That doesn't look so bad, Lena."

"What..." Startled, Lena turned to face the intruder. "What are you doing in my house, Roland?"

"I think you'll have to bind that; otherwise it won't close properly. May I?"

Lena took a step back, pulling her hand close to her chest. "I asked a question, Roland. What are you doing here?"

"After what happened to Ren, and you know, Hobs missing—I thought you might want a friend to talk with."

"Friend? Roland, your idea of being *your* friend is my not having any friends but you. What gives you the right to say who can and can't be my friends?" She punctuated each word, decisively poking her finger into Roland's chest.

"What have I done to wrong you?"

"Lena, I can't get you out of my mind. I sleep, and I dream of you. When I wake, I see your face. What do you expect me to do? I love you, Lena!" he blurted quickly.

Shocked that he had actually said the words, Lena looked anywhere but at Roland. She knew what she had to say, but didn't know how he would take it.

She took a calming breath before continuing, "Roland, I know you think you love me, but you don't. I have tried over and over to get it into your head that I don't share your feelings. How many times do I have to tell you this before you understand?"

When she looked up, Roland was directly in front of her. His proximity was frightening; he had never been this aggressive with her.

"What are you doing?"

"You will be my mate, Lena!" There was a slight hysterical edge to his voice. "And I will have what's mine."

Roland grabbed Lena, his hands tracing the curves of her body. The only thought she had was to scream with all her might, which is exactly what she did.

Abigail heard the screams as she left Jonaton's house. She knew in an instant the voice that had made them—LENA!

Breaking into a run, she ignored her friends as they poured out of their houses. The door was ajar when she reached home—finding Lena was the only thought on her mind as she burst through the open door. She barely noticed the others entering behind her.

Through the door to the kitchen, she could see Lena on the floor—blood covered her hand. She rushed to her side and fell to her knees; her hand rested on her neck, checking if she was all right. She was alive.

She cradled her chanting, "Lena, Lena, Lena" as tears of relief streamed down her face.

"What happened here?" She heard the firm voice of Jonaton from the other room and heard the murmur of someone answering, followed by Jonaton's entrance into the kitchen moments later.

"Oh my," he gasped. "Is Lena all right?"

"I'm not sure," Abigail replied, wiping the tears from her eyes. "I found her unconscious on the floor. I looks like she may have cut herself preparing dinner, but this bruise on her face…"

Jonaton took a rag and wet it in the sink. Moving back to Abigail's side, he bent over and washed the girl's face. "That is a nasty bruise. Maybe she fainted and hit her head? No, that doesn't explain her scream, now does it?"

Lena's eyes fluttered open. She buried her face into her mother's chest, sobs racking her tiny frame. "It was horrible…"

It was some time before they were able to glean the facts of what had happened.

"Tom. You, Lars, Ken, and Mick find Roland NOW. I want him in the council chambers. Drag him there if you have to."

"Yes, Jonaton."

He turned back to Lena and Abigail. "We need to move to the council room. This time not even Pol will be able to help Roland. First, let's bind your hand, shall we. We can't have you bleed out, now can we?"

Jonaton's grandfatherly tone helped to soothe Lena, and he tears ceased. Lena quietly nodded her assent and watched as her mother gathered what he required.

He and Abigail bound her hand with clean bandages, giving Lena a few extra minutes to further compose herself.

"Will you be okay walking, Lena?"

"I feel better, I can walk to the hall."

Jonaton helped Lena to her feet before offering her his arm. He was furious with Roland and realized that he had never been angrier in all his long years.

It took forty-five minutes before the men entered the council hall with Roland in hand. Pol entered right behind them.

"I asked you, what right do you have dragging my son here like this?"

"Orders. Now stay out of our way."

Looking around the room, Pol spotted Abigail and Jonaton already seated, waiting. In a chair prominently situated before the council table sat Lena – in the Chair of the Victim.

Pol's face drained of blood as he looked at the girl. He noted the bruising on her face, the tear streaks, the bandage wrapped hand, and with sinking realization he could picture what must have happened. Even with that picture, his resolution strengthened. He would not let anything happen to Roland.

"I will ask again, what is going on here? Why have you dragged Roland from my house like a criminal?"

"Silence Pol, take your place. The Chair of the Victim is occupied and you know the Rules of Discovery. The victim faces her peers and makes her claim. Then, and only then can the accused and his defenders speak. Now SIT." He waited until Pol sat. He held him with his steady gaze before he turning and silencing the assembled with "Let us begin."

He regarded Lena with tenderness as he said, "Lena tell us what happened."

Those in the room listened as Lena told of the events that had occurred, of finding Roland in her home, and how she had been violated by his inappropriate touches...

"Then I screamed. It was the only thing I could think to do. That only made Roland furious—his fist flew, knocking me back. My vision went blurry and I lost consciousness."

"LIES, I tried to help her."

"Quiet Roland, you will have your turn. Is there anything else, Lena?"

She shook her head slowly.

"Thank you, Lena." Raising his head, he pierced Roland with his gaze, "Roland, you stand accused of entering a home without invitation, of assault and unwelcome advances. Do you have anything to say in your defense?"

Roland started to speak but was interrupted by his father. "Before my son speaks in his defense, I have a few questions if I may. I would like to have some points clarified."

"You have that right as a member of the council," Jonaton affirmed.

"Lena, I am not sure we have a clear picture yet of everything that happened. You've made serious accusations but appear to have left some facts out."

"No sir, I told exactly what happened."

"Have you? Fine, let's start with your hand. You haven't explained how you cut yourself. I couldn't help but notice the blood on the bandages," Pol pointed to the hand Lena's cradled.

With a glance down to her hands, Lena proceeded to recount her accident with the knife, and how she had been cleaning the blood from the wound when she discovered Roland there.

"Is it possible that you mistook his concern for you in your distress as inappropriate advances?" Pol asked quietly.

"NO! His actions were not those of concern. He ran his filthy hands up and down my body in ways I didn't like or want."

"Jonaton, I must protest her outburst. We are here to decide Roland's involvement, yet here she sits verbally assaulting him."

"Lena, please keep your comments to just the facts."

"Roland, tell us what happened," Pol asked as he sat down.

Roland cleared his throat. "First—my feelings for Lena are no secret, as many in town well know. My only mistake tonight was being in her house. I was nervous and excited and it got the best of me. You see, I wanted to ask her to enter into union with me."

Gasps greeted his pronouncement.

"After her overreaction, I don't think I want that anymore. I'm not sure why or how, but I must have frightened her because the knife slipped and she cut her hand. She was looking at her hand when she screamed, I think it may have been in frustration at what she had done." Roland directed his gaze to look directly at Jonaton. "Since it was clear she didn't want me there, I left. I never touched her. That's the truth of it."

As he sat down, Jonaton asked a single question. "So what is your explanation for the bruise on her face? She has stated you struck her for screaming."

It was Pol who answered. "In what condition did you find her when you arrived?"

Abigail, with a new hatred of Pol, answered with venom in her voice, "Unconscious on the floor."

"Then isn't it equally possible that she fainted from the cut and loss of blood, striking her head on the counter when she fell?"

"She said Roland struck her and made unwanted advances..." Abigail started.

"So says Lena—the same girl who threatened Roland yesterday when she interrupted a fight between him and Hobs. A fight that Hobs started, if I might add."

"That's not how it was at all—Roland was angry that Hobs was speaking to me yesterday morning, and wanted to teach Hobs a lesson. Roland, Cades, and Piers were beating him before I interrupted them," Lena stated with passion.

"That is not how I heard it from Roland," Pol paused before continuing, "or from Cades and Piers."

Turning to the assembled, "We have heard accusation yet there are no witnesses. Instead there is only Lena's word and Roland's defense. She is clearly distraught by the loss of her friend and I think she has blown this situation out of proportion. I move for charges to be dismissed, and this matter settled."

Jonaton sighed. Pol had already covered Roland's discretion with his obfuscation and he was disrupting the purpose of this meeting.

"Enough! We have heard enough to know that Roland by his own admission entered a house without welcome. Regarding the question of the assault, as there are no additional witnesses we will defer it for now." The triumphant smile on Pol's face made Jonaton continue.

"However, this indiscretion will be noted in the records in the event of future indiscretions."

Pol jumped to his feet. "You can't do this! Nothing has been proven."

Jonaton knew exactly what he was doing. He would eliminate Roland from ever taking a seat on the council.

"It is done. By your sons own admission he was in Lena's home without an invitation." Jonaton turned to face Roland, locking his gaze upon him. "Regarding the invasion of Lena's privacy, you are commanded to the following punishment. You will complete three months of menial labor. Since we no longer have a grazer tender, you will take those responsibilities as yours. Council, do you concur?"

"YES," Abigail stated immediately.

After a long pause Pol added, "Yes."

Jonaton, sensing Abigail trembling beside him, placed a hand gently on her shoulder in an attempt to calm her.

With a crash of his gavel, he closed the meeting with a resounding finality.

"Abigail, can you and Lena stay a moment?" Jonaton asked as everyone started to file out of the hall.

"How could you do this Jonaton," Abigail demanded, turning on him with betrayal in her eyes.

Jonaton sighed deeply. "Abigail, after a few years you will understand. We must have undeniable facts before we can sentence anyone. By his own admission, Roland violated Lena's privacy by entering the house. However, Pol and Roland cast enough doubt on the story that if we sentenced him for assault then people would question our right to lead, and then where would we be? We must at all times portray ourselves as impartial leaders, and worthy of the positions we hold.

"By our ruling here today we have denied that which Pol most wanted—his son Roland on the council. Further, we have hopefully prevented further assaults on Lena since it is now a matter of record. A single accusation and Roland can be sentenced for both crimes."

He could see the anger slowly melt from Abigail's face.

Turning to Lena he asked, "You are all right, aren't you, Lena, my dear?"

She nodded yes. "Jonaton, he was lying regarding Hobs. They would have killed him if I didn't stop them yesterday – Roland was furious with Hobs; I have never seen him so angry before. For all I know, they might have followed him and finished what they started!"

Jonaton raised a warning hand. "Be careful with your accusations young lady; they can be held against you in council if you say them to the wrong people. We will find out what happened to Hobs, don't you worry," he concluded.

Chapter 10

Archon quietly observed Hobs, monitoring his progress as he worked through the lessons that he had been given. The boy had a voracious appetite to learn, asking questions that yearned for answers. Once he grasped the full impact of was being presented, he asked Archon to teach him more—a request that Archon was more than willing to fulfill.

While Hobs slept that night, Archon pondered on why Hobs had fainted earlier—after careful review of the medical scans, he determined it was simply the result of sensory overload. He had been provided too much information too fast without the base to properly process what he was learning; therefore, this morning Archon decided to alter his approach.

"Hobs. To prevent what happened yesterday, I would like to structure a more *formal* training program for you."

Hobs, who had been eating, paused. "Huh? What do you mean? What will I be learning?"

"Anything you desire, as I said yesterday; however, I think it would be wise to start with the basics. You need to have a solid foundation if you are to have a proper understanding of the lessons that you are learning. I propose to give you the basic education that all Valaran children received starting at age four. From that foundation we can continue on through the specialized training they received in their teenage years."

"And this training will help me understand these words jumbled in my head?"

"In a word, *yes*. I will give you the knowledge in manageable chunks. As you access and process this information, you will start to gain comprehension – that is where your learning will truly begin. After each upload, I will test you on the materials learned in order to ensure that you understand the lessons.

You should be able to proceed rapidly through the beginning courses—shall we begin?"

"Let's."

And so it began. Archon started with the fourth-year training and progressed from there. True to his word, after each upload Archon tested Hobs on his grasp of the information and in its practical applications.

Hobs didn't miss a question. The more he learned, the more he wanted to learn. He was insatiable.

By midmorning he had a firm grasp on the fundamentals: math, science, art, music, history, martial arts – all with much improved comprehension. He was forming challenging questions that yesterday would have been impossible. Archon was pleased with the results. By the conclusion of the eighth-year material, Archon had to call a stop.

Hobs was a machine, wanting more and more knowledge. "This is enough for the day, Hobs. You require food, followed by a workout. It is important that we stimulate and strengthen the body as well as the brain."

"But I want to know more about these mathematical equations we were working on, just a bit more." Hobs pleaded as he turned back to the equations in question.

In response, Archon deactivated the terminal where he was seated, clearly terminating the pleading as well. "Tomorrow."

"As you wish." Hobs stood with a sigh of disappointment.

Archon followed his progress as Hobs went in search of food. When he finished eating, Archon ordered him to the training facility to work off his excess energy.

Hobs finished a strenuous workout with the weight equipment and wiped the sweat from his face with his towel. The workout had been good for him. He felt relaxed yet alert.

"Archon, I'm sorry."

"For what?"

"You were correct, I needed this. I feel much better now. So—thank you."

"You are quite welcome Hobs."

He cast his gaze around the training facility, noting things he hadn't understood before. The weapon rack on the far wall captured his attention, and walking over he examined the various hand-to-hand weapons it contained. With care, he selected a beautiful sword he recalled being named a Kal'Tel.

The Kal'Tel was a slightly curved blade just under a meter in length, ending at a two-handed hilt. Ornate metalwork where the hilt met the blade offered protection to the wielder's hands. Hobs accessed his new memories, able to recall bits of information regarding the sword's construction.

The Kal'Tel was made by hand, its blade folded over and over as it was crafted. The end result of the process was an extremely sharp, durable blade.

As years passed and technology grew, the blade itself was modified to include "tech" into the core of the blade. A notch had been cut into the blade, running three-quarters of its the length. This notch started at the hilt, giving the appearance that there were two blades that seamlessly came together just below the tip. In the notch was tech that emitted an energy force that infused the blade, making it a hundred times more lethal than naked steel would have been. When activated, the blade would glow with a faint halo in one of a variety of colors – the color would indicate the rank of the maker of the Kal'Tel; blue tech was the created by a master, green by an expert and so on. Beyond his knowledge of the various color the tech itself confused Hobs; the information he possessed didn't delve deeper into that aspect of the weapon.

It was the weapon of a master and as such had a full gamut of rituals and customs that the student of the blade adhered to.

He "*remembered*" exercises with the sword and decided to practice what he remembered. Kal'Tel in hand, he stepped out onto the mat and executed a formal bow, bringing the weapon to ready.

He dropped into a defensive stance, followed with a double attack, ending with a parry against an attacker coming from the side. He tucked the blade and dropped into a roll, evading a strike from behind while rising into another double attack. He continued with attack, block, parry, roll until he completed the full routine.

Breathing heavily with the exertion, Hobs respectfully replaced the Kal'Tel in the weapon rack before returning to his room.

"Archon, I am ready," Hobs stated the following morning. Sitting at his terminal he carefully inserting the uplink cable into the data port exactly as Archon had taught him.

"Before we begin, another test," was Archon's reply.

Hobs groaned in protest. "You and your tests. Do we have to?"

"Tests allow me to assess whether you have properly grasped the material you are learning. If you demonstrate the proper recall and comprehension of yesterday's material then we will proceed. If not, then I will be required to modify your learning plan. Shall we begin?"

With a sigh, Hobs answered, "Yes Archon, *you're* in charge."

Ignoring the sarcasm, Archon launched into an exhaustive test that covered material from all four years Hobs had learned the previous day. Hobs answered each question without hesitation, not a single one wrong.

"Very good, Hobs. Let us begin the next phase of your training," Archon concluded.

"Finally," Hobs muttered under his breath, knowing but not caring that Archon could still hear him.

Archon uploaded ninth-year training, followed again by extensive testing. This was the routine he followed for the balance of the morning, uploading years ten, eleven, and twelve.

"That is enough for today. You have now completed the basic early Valaran education. From this point forward we will focus on specialized training. At the rate you are proceeding, you can learn as many specializations as you would like."

"Whatever I like?"

"I believe that is what I just told you."

"I want it all, science, mathematics, medicine, music, engineering, flight training..."

Hobs could almost hear laughter in Archon's voice as he interrupted him. "All that you ask and more shall be yours, young Hobs. Following the precedent set yesterday the morning will be spent learning; your afternoons will be spent in fitness and combat training; time in the evening will be for whatever you wish to pursue."

"Based on your interest in the Kal'Tel yesterday, I have included training with that weapon in your uploads, I will release it to you now, along with advanced self-defense training."

As if a switch were flipped, Hobs could now access the promised information.

"I have to learn how you do that, Archon." Hobs paused, considering how to continue, "I have a question though—why all the combat training?"

"All in good time young Hobs, all in good time. Suffice it to say, I require you to be able to properly defend yourself. Now off, eat some lunch and enjoy your afternoon workout."

Archon was pleased. The final test for the morning had taken Hobs an hour to complete, but his recall was perfect. Archon crafted his tests in such a way that they worked on comprehension and not just recall. The only conclusion that Archon could come to was that Hobs had a phenomenal mind, and the term genius was not far from being accurate.

"Why do you have to be so stubborn? I just want to learn a few more things."

"You have been taught enough for the day, young Hobs. I will not risk another overload." After his workout, Hobs had returned to working on advanced mathematics equations and showed signs of frustration.

"Why not!?!"

"I am not one to be manipulated by a petulant child. Enough is enough, good night."

"Archon?" After a long pause, "Archon? Fine, ignore me...argh!"

Archon was obviously not going to give in no matter how much Hobs whined. He did not, however, turn the terminal off which surprised Hobs.

After grabbing a hot beverage called tea, he decided to try and gather information from the terminal on his own. He had learned so much today, but everything he learned just created more questions to which Hobs wanted answers. He paused, not sure where to start—the terminal was voice-activated, but you first had to have an idea what information you wanted to know.

Hobs tucked his feet up under him before addressing the terminal. "Tell me about this place."

"The facility you are currently located in is designated Station Alpha. You are here..." the computer provided a map with his current location in the facility, along with the various places Hobs had access to go. It wasn't the information that Hobs was looking for so he interrupted the playback.

"No, tell me about this world," he tried again.

"Detailed or overview?"

"Overview please."

"The world known as Cygnus Prime was first incorporated into the Valaran Empire 1200 cycles ago based on the current revolutions of the planet. The inhabitants of Cygnus Prime welcomed the Valaran with open arms, embracing the knowledge they could learn from them and how it would improve their planet.

"No longer were they plagued with the wars that had once raged among the various nations of the time. Education increased as the Cygnian sent their children to the education centers. Over time Cygnus became a major military base for the Valaran forces situated on the edge of the Valaran Empire, which resulted in the installation of Archon to oversee the facility.

"Two hundred years after the Valaran arrived the Scarian declared war on Valara. They revolted in a bloody civil war, ruthless in their campaign – it wasn't long before the Scarian armada attacked this planet.

"They leveled the cities into rumble, murdering anyone who stood in their path. Many Cygnian died that day, and the Valaran were all but eradicated. The Scarian were ruthless and determined to see that no Valaran remained alive.

"The people of Cygnus Prime were forced to live an almost primitive existence. Yet some knowledge was retained over the years, and it has only been recently that have we seen the expansion of towns and the gathering of survivors..."

"Stop playback," He knew about his world, as it existed today. He wanted to know something else. "Tell me about the Scarian."

"Detailed or overview?"

"For this session unless I specify detailed, default to overview."

"Preference noted and saved."

"The Scarian are originally from the planet known as Scaria. Before the Valaran subjugated them, they had spread throughout ten star systems, destroying the populations to obtain control of the planets. Their mistake was conquering a Valaran planet in this manner.

"The Scarian are reptilian in origin and as such are cold-blooded. They reproduce by laying eggs, which are placed in hatcheries where a working class cares for them until they hatch. Once the young are hatched they are indoctrinated in the Scarian war college until they are ready to take their place in the armies of the juggernaut.

"The Scarian are a warlike race, constantly fighting among their various clans in skirmishes which long kept their population under control. They came to the attention of Valara when they decimated the population of a colony world. The Valaran did not know that the planet was claimed by the Scarian when they settled it.

"Rather than retaliating against the Scarian, the Valaran only subjugated them, thinking that they could bring them to enlightenment. They had no desire to destroy a sentient race—this was their biggest mistake. The Scarian pretended to accept their overlords, while secretly building ships and amassing their forces.

"After ten years of preparation, they struck back. The Scarian had carefully planned their assaults targeting shipyards, bases, and major training facilities. After those were dealt with, they began their genocide of the Valaran civilization."

"Pause," Hobs softly said.

He stared at the picture of the Scarian on the screen. The image was of a bipedal reptilian creature, with scales ranging in color from yellow to green covering the body. The caption indicated that they stood two and a half meters in height. Muscles rippled in the arms and legs, both ending with three lethal-looking claws. The Scarian was clothed in a shipsuit, its short tail jutting out from an opening in the back. A snout thrust out from its head, with ear holes on either side and piercing orbs of black perched over the snout. Razor-sharp teeth were evident; it looked as if the Scarian appeared to be—smiling?

A shudder coursed through Hobs' body. The creature looked evil. What had caused them to be so vicious? He wondered.

He had seen enough. It was getting late and he was feeling tired and wanted to relax. Settling back in his chair, Hobs stretched, carefully working the kinks from his neck and shoulders.

"Archon had been monitoring Hobs and noted the mental fatigue settling in, "Hobs you must rest now; otherwise you may relapse," Archon said with concern.

"Now you're back, geez."

"I was never gone, you were acting inappropriately."

"Whatever."

"Never forget, the computer systems are always at your command. When I am not providing your instruction, you can discover how stimulating it is to learn for yourself. I trust that what you learned satisfied some of your curiosity?"

"I guess… No, you are right of course. Finding the information for myself was a good exercise. I think I'm already becoming too accustomed to the fast-track learning."

"There will come a time when your fast-track learning will no longer be available; when that time comes you must be able to use what you have learn and expand upon it."

"I understand." Hobs paused thinking about what he wanted to do, "Archon, I was wondering..."

"Yes?"

"I saw a music room on the map earlier, does it have a piano? I would like to try some of the music theory you've been teaching me."

"There is one there, would you like me to dispatch X08 to take you?"

"I think I can find my way, plus the walk will give me time to think."

"As you wish."

Hobs left his room and crossed the training facility to the exit. The music room was only a few corridors away and he was surprised when he found himself before a door labeled stage entrance. He entered and found a Grand Piano prominently placed on a stage in the front of the large room; as he looked out from the stage he could make out seating forming a semi-circle with each row higher than the one in front – he could make out eight rows in all.

He moved to the piano and sat down – Archon had included music and theory in his training but Hobs had yet to play an instrument other then a recorder.

There was a musical score open on the piano – Battle Hymn of Valara. Without knowing more than that it was proper to do so, Hobs reviewed the score before attempting to play the piece. He was extremely clumsy in his first attempt, missing note after note, causing him to grow more and more frustrated; Archon had explained that certain skills required muscle memory that only came with years of practice – he could see that Archon was correct, yet that didn't deter him from playing the piece again.

By the fifth time through he was almost ready to call it quits as he slammed his clenched fist onto the keys in frustration. It was much easier demonstrating combat moves or completing calculus equation than it was playing the piano.

He decided to run through it one more time; this time he concentrated on feeling the rhythm and flow of the piece, he was still making quite a few mistakes but it was a better performance. He forced his breath out in a long sigh and considered the simple beauty of the music that he had just completed.

"That was well played Hobs." Archon broke the silence with sincerity, and what appeared to be longing, in his voice. "With practice you will get much better."

"It was terrible, I *know* what I should be playing, but my fingers don't want to do what I want – like here in the fourth movement," Hobs rifled through the score to find the part in question.

"Don't criticize yourself; music is complex and encompasses many skills. You cannot expect to be a virtuoso on your first day."

Archon allowed the silence to hang for a few seconds before continuing; "You have made tremendous strides in your training in a short period of time. I know that the past few days have been hard for you, and that you are struggling with all the new things you are learning. My role is not only to provide knowledge, but also to train you in ways to acquire additional knowledge on your own, using more traditional methods of learning if you will – take learning to play music for example. While you *know* the theory and technique it is quite another thing to put that into practice."

"Tell me about it," Hobs muttered, still discouraged.

Archon considered his next words carefully, "You do not have to be *perfect* when you play as long as you *feel* the emotion in the music. There were master who could play that score perfectly yet lacked the ability to evoke emotion with it as you just did."

Hobs blushed at the compliment, feeling his frustration melt away. "Thanks."

"Promise me one thing Hobs."

"What?"

"If you chose to continue with you pursuit of music, strive to learn, but do not allow your pursuit of perfection to mar your music – allow your feelings to be expressed when you play."

"I think I understand what you mean and I promise to try." Hobs paused before continue, "Is there anymore music that I can practice?"

"You can print whatever you desire from the databanks. Now however it is late and it think that it would be wise for you to get some rest."

"Would it be possible for me to find time to practice each night?"

"If that is your wish, yes. It is good to hear music in these halls once more – you have made me feel young again, and for that I thank you."

"You are welcome Archon." Hobs rose from the piano and returned to his room.

Archon monitored him, noting the exhaustion that had settled in. With a single command, he sent instructions for a warm beverage with a mild sedative to be ready in the food unit.

"I have prepared a beverage to help you rest," Archon said with concern as Hobs entered his room.

"Thank you," Hobs dutifully took the drink and drank it swiftly.

Archon lowered the lights after Hobs lay on the bed; as the room darkened he queried, "Archon?"

"Yes," Archon replied.

"There's something you aren't telling me, isn't there?" Hobs questioned.

Archon realized that if he lied at this time Hobs would see right through it. "Yes there is, young Hobs, and you are almost ready to hear it."

Archon waited to see if Hobs would push the point, but all he heard was soft breathing. Hobs had fallen asleep. Soon he would have to be told everything, including his heritage, Archon concluded as he returned to the preparations.

Archon had been busy since the probe had detected his facility— the wealth of his knowledge had to be saved no matter the cost. Activating a facility deep in the southern mountains, he began running numerous diagnostics. While they were running, he verified that the connections between this facility and it were still stable. They were!

While Hobs was working out in the afternoon, Archon had spent the time transferring information from his databanks to the storage units there. Reserve power in the facility was sufficient to keep the data safe for thousands of years. He had a wealth of knowledge that was too valuable to be lost if Valara was to rise from the ashes.

The final part of his plan was to store a copy of his programming there so that it could be reactivated in the future if needed. Of course, there would be the loss of any knowledge from the point of transfer until reactivation, but that was as it must be. There would also be the loss of who he, Archon, was in his essence—at the core of his being.

He ran the probabilities over and over, and it was inevitable that this facility would be destroyed. He knew that the Scarian would be on their way as soon as the message was received on Scaria. War drones were activated and preparation begun in hangars buried deep under the frozen ice caps to the north. They wouldn't be much use against an armada, but he planned to do as much devastation as he could to their forces while defending this planet.

After reviewing what had been covered in Hobs' training to this point, Archon started formulated what he would teach for the balance of the week. He also considered what he could upload into Hobs' brain for the future.

The future—everything depended on Hobs' consent, but the future was looking good.

He would have to tell Hobs everything he knew. It was no longer speculation; Archon knew that what he would tell Hobs was fact. The evidence confirmed it, and for the first time in quite a long time, Archon knew there was hope.

Starting tomorrow he would begin teaching Hobs various engineering disciplines, stellar navigation, and the piloting of ground, air, and spacecraft. He would provide advanced medical and combat training that would round off what he knew Hobs would require. It was unfair to Hobs that he would be pushed to excel at the martial skills at a rapid pace without the proper time for his body to adjust to the new skills, but there was no other option; Hobs must be able to defend himself – everything else, such as music, would have to fit where it could.

With that done he turned his attention to his core. Analysis scans had detected decay there and it was accelerating at a fast rate. Even without the Scarian threat he would only have a limited number of centuries left. If that!

Yes, tomorrow, he would tell Hobs everything.

Chapter 11

The long, cylindrical shape slowly rotated in space, fixed in a geosynchronous orbit above a dead moon. Light from the distant sun faintly reflected off the matte black surface. Lights twinkled in the blackness of space along the length the cylinder, and heavy plasteel windows dotted its surface offering eyes out to the void.

The position of the station was far enough from the sun to avoid interference with its primary function—listening for messages. The listening post had been hanging in this orbit for years on end and would remain in place for a thousand more. It had started its long existence as a Valaran outpost; now it provided intel for the Scarian juggernaut.

Within the station, computers performed tasks that they had been programmed to complete with silent precision. Circuits and relays opened and closed in their timeless dance as they had for centuries. Yet day after day the results were the same—silence; that was until today.

Alone, in the cold dark station, a pair of eyes that were fully alien scanned the equipment banks. Brood Warrior Ssplin had been stationed on this desolate outpost for fifteen revolutions around the local sun. A lifetime away from the swamplands of Scaria, and his mate! Stationed—that was a joke. More like sentenced to the station as an outcast! Here on the edge of nowhere with nothing but his brooding to fill the long nights.

What was there to defend against? The Valaran war was long over; any glory as a warrior was now found in victory over the other clans. Clan Vrang, his clan, had been in power since the fall of Valara, and his had been dreams of keeping things that way. He was a warrior!

His hopes had been high – they had included dreams of laying eggs with Znissa and of seeing his young grow into strong warriors of the empire. One mistake of judgment and here he was, wiping the asses of lizards not long out of the shell. He was commander of a command that would lead to nowhere.

It was only due to his father's position as Sub Commander of the War Council that Ssplin had not been summarily executed. Instead he was banished to an existence of mediocrity. Relegated to tasks that even the dullest-witted warrior could manage – all because of one error in judgment!

Thinking back, he should have killed those five females on Reagnus—he still contemplated why he hadn't to this day. Was it because they had all been mothers? Or mothers soon to be?

Try as he might, Ssplin couldn't think of any logical reason other than that to have spared their lives, yet he had! He even went as far as preventing his squad from killing them. That had been his only mistake.

Ssplin closed his eyes—part of his punishment had been to watch as each warrior under his command was executed at the hand of his father! *His own father* – as an expression of his disappointment and disgust with his son he had carried out the death sentences.

Ssplin had trained with those warriors. He had introduced two of them to their mates. He had been there when their sons had broken the shell and entered life. Now, he thought bitterly, now their mates wouldn't even look at him. They had spit and hissed at him as he was led off to the transport bound for hell! Hell was the station he was now in charge of.

He laughed the way Scarian did with a slight hissing sound—yet it held an edge of frustration. In charge? Of what?

The soldiers under his command were little better than criminals. Do a good job, file reports on time, and they were rewarded with enough food until the next cycle of reports was expected. Do a poor job, and—well, the food wasn't delivered, and soon there was one less soldier. It was the natural cycle of life onboard the station.

Since Ssplin had assumed charge, he had managed to only lose two warriors. These had been replaced shortly after with two more *drazsdins*, failures!

Yet even here, in the back end of space, Ssplin demanded a high level of obedience. He was accustomed to unfaltering obedience as one of the privileges of command, and his punishments for disobedience were harsh. He might be an outcast now, but he would succeed in rejoining the elite of the Scarian Warriors. It would only be a matter of time.

A wicked grin split his muzzle as he contemplated his return to Scaria; his father would pay with his life as the final mark of his exiled son's return. He would pay for the soldiers he had slaughtered without remorse; Znissa would rue the day that she turned her back on him; the war council would pay for what they did to him.

Early on he had identified two warriors worthy of being his War Masters. The War Masters each in turn oversaw a Hand; a Hand was a squad comprised of five warriors.

Warriors—he could only use that term loosely, but Ssplin had been ruthlessly drilling "his" troops, expecting nothing but the best and he was slowly seeing the results he expected. A firm hand was all they required, and swift punishment for disobedience.

Raising his muzzle up from his musings, he looked out through the one-way window of his office into the control center. He always maintained two warriors on duty during the 'night' cycles – night, who was to say what was night? There was no night in space, yet they maintained their schedule according to Scaria's rotation so this was their *night*.

He had spent the entire evening in his office completing his review of intel reports – they were to go out in the morning only to state that there was nothing new to report. It wasn't often that he was able to review the performance of his night crew and he wasn't satisfied with their performance – they were not as *attentive* as they should be. With a closer glance, he determined that one of his warriors was actually sleeping. He was a new *recruit* and hadn't learned how things worked around here—that would soon change.

With grim determination Ssplin rose to his feet. After checking that his blaster was properly holstered and his uniform perfectly in place he opened the door and entered the control room.

The warrior who was awake jumped to his feet in response to the opening of the office door, instantly snapping to attention after a quick kick of his partner's chair. "Sir."

"*Shells*," he cursed at the first warrior before slowly looked around. A look of shock lit his eyes when he saw Brood Warrior Ssplin standing in the room. He snapped to attention ignoring his rumpled uniform. "Sir."

Ssplin ignored their response, forcing them to remain at attention where they cast nervous glances at one another. They had been unaware that Ssplin was in his office when they came on duty – the prior watch had failed to inform them of this important fact.

But he had been there the entire shift, quietly reviewing the reports for headquarters. It was deadly silent as he walked over to the communications station and opened the channel they used for station-wide announcements.

He turned to face the two warriors as he commenced his broadcast to the station. "At three hundred hours station time Warrior Sszirtne was found sleeping at his post." With a move quicker than Sszirtne could react to, Ssplin opened his throat with a quick swipe of his claws.

Sszirtne fell to the floor and with shock in his eyes he gazed at the pool of amber blood slowly spreading beneath him as he struggled to cling to life.

Warrior Tsaf watched on in horror not noticing that Ssplin had un-holstered his blaster and was aiming it at him.

"Further," Ssplin continued, "for allowing this dereliction of duty, I sentence Warrior Tsaf to death."

With a sickening realization of what was about to happen, he slowly turned to Ssplin in order to plead his case – this action resulted in Tsaf receiving the full discharge of the blaster in his face, vaporizing his head in an instant.

Sszirtne watched the headless mass of his Tsaf hit the ground as the spark of his life faded into extinction.

"War Masters Sszlont and Prissng to my office immediately," Ssplin ordered into the still-open communications channel.

After closing the connection, he returned the mic to the console. As he sat to wait for their arrival he noticed the flashing telltale on the console indicating a transmission. Strange, he thought as he moved to the screen. He retrieved the waiting message and glanced at the header of the transmission. No messages had been received from that sector in over eight hundred cycles. Toggling the playback, he watched the message scroll by, eyes widening in surprise.

This would be his opportunity for redemption. It would be his ticket for getting out of this hellhole once and for all. He settled back, quietly waiting for his War Masters.

War Masters Sszlont and Prissng knew better than to keep the Broad Warrior waiting and they entered the control center within minutes. They had paused just long enough to waken their Hands and issue orders for them to assemble outside the command center.

Ssplin would be in a foul mood tonight after this gross dereliction of duty, they thought as they entered the control center. They were surprised to see that it wasn't the case at all. In fact, he appeared quite excited about something.

"Reporting as ordered, sir," the two announced as they snapped to attention.

Ssplin turned to face his War Masters. "The gods smile upon us this night, and we are favored," he stated to his surprised warriors. "But first, deal with these—*things*," Ssplin commanded with a dismissive wave of his hand, indicating the two dead warriors.

Prissng moved to the door and issued orders to the remaining members of his squad waiting outside. "You two clean this mess now—remove the bodies to food reclamation."

He watched as his warriors jumped to complete their assigned task; he was fearful of the consequences since the two dead warriors had been under his command. What would his punishment be?

The three watched as the warriors removed the two bodies, the door whooshing shut behind them.

They were surprised to hear Ssplin's hissing laugh before he continued, "Eating will be good for a while now I think." Then, returning to the issue at hand, "Read this transmission," he ordered.

Sszlont and Prissng read the transmission, and then read it again. This couldn't be! Valaran energy signatures after all this time and— they paused, checking the transmission's origin—from such a remote location.

Sszlont was the first to recover. "Fortune has indeed smiled on us," he hissed. "We must notify high command immediately."

Ssplin cut him off short. "NO!" he exclaimed with a hiss of wrath. "If we send this on to high command then they will take all the glory and piss on us. WE," he paused as he motioned to the three of them, "we will investigate this anomaly and deal with it accordingly." Ssplin held both of them in his iron gaze. "Then we will have the glory with the result being our return to the places of honor for which we were bred!"

The finality in his voice was such that both Sszlont and Prissng knew there would be no arguing with him.

"Make the assault craft ready Sszlont," he commanded with a dismissive wave of his hand.

Sszlont and Prissng saluted him – bringing their right hands to their heart before turning to leave. They were brought short as Ssplin continued, "And Prissng, another mistake like this and you will join your warriors as food, am I understood."

The chill in Ssplin's voice pierced to Prissng's core. He nodded, acknowledging the threat knowing that Ssplin would carry through with his threat if he failed again.

"You will continue with your hand two warriors short until such time as we receive replacements. I will not punish Sszlont for your failure. Further, I require one of your warriors to man this station while preparations are underway." Ssplin ended with finality.

Sszlont ordered his squad to the hangar double time. He would make certain that he had the assault craft ready in record time.

Though not ordered to do so, Prissng knew it was his task to make sure the expedition's weapons and ordnance were ready. With his three warriors returning from the burial duty, he ordered one to man the comm station, while informing the remaining warriors to follow him. The two bodies were already being processed into dry rations, some of which they would take on this voyage.

Ssplin grinned with satisfaction at the response from his War Masters as he returned to his office. Another lesson learned he thought with pleasure – but would he have enough warriors for the mission at hand? He would find out soon enough.

But now there were tasks to complete; he had to prepare the station for automated operations. In the slim chance that someone would choose to communicate with the station he would make sure that the communications would be forwarded to the assault craft. The sender would notice an increased delay, but Ssplin would use the excuse of a faulty relay station. One that he had rigged to 'fail' in the event that he needed such an excuse.

He pulled up the stellar charts for the Cygnus region and calculated transit times at near light; the journey would take just over a week – this would mean cyro suspension and while he hated being put under it was a necessary evil; without it the trip would take much longer. If he had a destroyer under his command they would be able to manage the trip and remain awake. If, and more ifs – all this would change soon.

He saved his calculations for the journey before downloading them to the assault craft.

Satisfied that everything was in order, Ssplin departed for his chambers to prepare himself for the mission; it wouldn't be long now before he would be returned to his former glory and command. He would simply have to wait a few more weeks.

Chapter 12

Bitterness and anger raged through Roland as he rose before the sun. It was all so unfair, he thought. He had a punishment to complete, for what? Trying to tell Lena how he felt? Thoughts that had previously been of want and desire had swiftly turned to a raging hate and loathing of her over the past few days since the council had pronounced their judgment – that his father had agreed with them hurt even more.

Lena, what a bitch she had turned out to be. With one scream she had ruined all of his plans and goals for his life.

Was it so wrong to want her as his mate?

Without taking even a moment to consider what he was offering her, she had rejected him!

His thoughts were a swirl of rage; Hobs—he was the root of all his failures. If he found Hobs there would be an account to settle. Roland would make sure Hobs never interfered in his life again. No matter what anyone else believed he didn't think Hobs was dead. They hadn't found a body when they searched the knoll and they should have.

But where was he?

Finding his gear, but not finding Hobs was a puzzle—he didn't like things he couldn't solve.

Roland made his way slowly to the grazer pens, shaking slightly in the brisk, cold morning air. He would take them back to Deadmans Knoll. He would spend the day searching for anything that would answer his questions. He would find Hobs, and then he would make him pay—oh yes, Hobs would pay dearly.

He glanced over to Abigail's house and saw the lights already on. He contemplated why they were up so early then the realization hit him – it was their washing day, a responsibility that Lena would undertake now that her mother was on the council.

He turned back to his charges – god the gazers smelled awful. They were dumb animals and it was beneath him to care for them but almighty Jonaton had commanded and now Roland had to complete the punishment meted out to him.

He would get even with Jonaton in time also. Roland wasn't sure how yet, but he would.

A sound from his left made him turn quickly. *Could a howler pack have actually entered town?* He wondered fearfully. "Who's there?"

As he scanned the shadows he watched two shapes slowly emerge in the dim morning. Not walking on four legs, as he had feared, but two. Roland breathed a sigh of relief. Man was he on edge this morning, and all because of that worthless bitch.

"Hey Rol," Piers began quietly, "Cades and I wanted to know if you would like us to hang with you today. You know, give you some company."

"Yeah, man, friends stick together."

Roland looked at Piers and Cades with an idea slowly forming in his mind. An idea that, while chilling on the surface, gave him a grim satisfaction that spread like warmth through his body. An idea that he knew both of his friends would help with since they were already accomplices in what happened to Ren. They would have no choice but to help him with what he was planning, he would see to that.

He drew his friends closer and explained what he wanted them to do. He watched as a look of horror crossed both of his friends' faces.

"We can't do that Rol." Piers vehemently objected.

Roland silenced anything Cades was about to add with a glare. Cades would do whatever he told him to do; Piers would take a bit of persuading. "You will do this for me. You are both guilty in Ren's death and if you don't help me then the council might just found out that both of you were guilty of his death."

"You wouldn't." Cades gasped, his face turning white as a sheet.

"I will if you don't do what I want." He watched as their reluctance slowly turn to acceptance.

"We'll do it," Piers conceded with his head bowed.

His eyes followed as Piers and Cades rushed to get away; he knew that they wouldn't fail him. They wouldn't risk the consequences; he also knew that if he had allowed them to think about it they would have realized that he would have been condemning himself along with them – no matter, he knew without a doubt that they would do exactly as he had outlined. With a wicked grin on his face he turned and opened the gate to the pen before leading the grazers out into the chill morning. With deft commands, and some vicious prodding with his staff, he led them on the slow, long walk to Deadmans Knoll.

As they ran to get into place in order to put Roland's plan into motion, Piers put his thoughts into words, "He's gone too far this time Cades; what are we going to do?"

"Do?" Cades slowed to a walk in order to catch his breath. "We're going to do what he told us to do."

"But we didn't *do* anything wrong."

"Didn't we? We watch Ren die. Roland pushed him."

"He told the council that it was an accident."

"Was it though? You heard what Ren said the same as I did. He knew about how we beat Hobs that morning – how did he know that?"

"So you think Roland pushed him on purpose."

"You don't? Besides, how do we know he died in the fall?"

"Roland said…"

"Exactly, Roland said he was dead. What if he wasn't? What if Roland is heading there to make sure the job is finished?" Cades paused, "It doesn't really matter either way. Hobs was a pain in the ass and Ren coddled him. I say, good riddance to both of them."

Piers was cowered by the vehemence in his friends voice, "But what he's asking us to do is just as bad."

"And if we don't do it, what do you think Roland will do then?" Cades let the unspoken punishment hang in the air.

Piers hung his head, "I hope you know what you are doing."

"I do; we are helping our friend."

Piers fell silent – it was no use arguing with Cades. Roland had said it was an accident when it had happened and they believed him.

But what if it wasn't, what if Roland had meant to push him? That would be a different thing altogether. By the town law, the result of their silence would be that they were just as guilty as if they had pushed him – the punishment for murder was the life of the murderer. So if it hadn't been an accident, they were guilty. To make matters worse, it also would mean that they had participated in a lie to the council. There was no going back now. Neither of them wanted to die so they would help Roland.

They continued their trek to the river where they would wait for the inevitable. Piers debated in his mind the morality of his current dilemma; what if Ren's death had been exactly what had been argued, a horrible accident, and that they were guilty of no crime – what they were doing now would take them beyond the point of no return.

Abigail rose to make an early breakfast since she wanted to return to her study of the records – it was her new passion, one that was resulting in the discovery of so many fascinating things. The history of Redwood was compelling; one that spanned many generations as it chronicled the story of life and survival in the midst of adversity.

It was clear that Lena didn't understand what she found so interesting in the records, but Abigail could tell she was proud of her all the same. As she prepared their breakfast she could hear Lena beginning to stir in the bedroom. "Lena, breakfast."

Moments later Lena entered the room wiping sleep from her eyes. Abigail served their breakfast before seating herself at the table beside her.

"Lena I need to go to the Hall of Records again today. Would you be able to help with a few extra chores this morning?" Abigail hated asking this of her daughter since she already did so much around the house, but with her new responsibilities she did need the help.

Lena regarded her with a bright, infectious smile that lit the room. "Of course, Mother. Anything to help." Lena sprang up and gave her mother a quick hug, "I'm so proud of you."

Abigail returned the smile as she watched Lena return to her seat, "It's just one extra chore really—after you finish with the laundry I would like it if you would stop over to clean Jonaton's house. You know how frail he has been of late and I want to help him as much as possible."

"No problem," Lena replied. "Besides, it won't take all that long. He keeps his place quite clean."

"Thanks all the same Lena. I will tell Jonaton to expect you this afternoon."

They finished breakfast in companionable conversation, then rose and quickly cleaned the kitchen, each preparing for the day ahead.

Lena finished and headed to her room to get dressed; Abigail headed for the door with a promise to see her later in the evening.

Lena carefully locked the door and picked up the basket of laundry. She enjoyed taking care of the laundry as it was peaceful by the river and the chore gave her plenty of time to think.

Turning, she greeted her neighbors as she made her way to the town gates. Her thoughts were a roiling turmoil as she walked. The root cause of it all came down to whom she would enter into the Union with. Roland wanted her—he had made abundantly clear the week prior; but something had changed. He was *hostile* towards her now. Regardless of what he felt, she wanted nothing to do with him.

For that matter, she didn't want Hobs for a mate either. They were best friends; she liked him and could tell him anything but her heart belonged to Mick – he was blissfully unaware of her attentions and did not return the feelings...yet.

She was working on changing that by taking every opportunity she could to be near him; she was starting to think that the attention she was paying him was starting to work. He had actually smiled back at her yesterday when they spoke. Her heart had felt like it would burst from her chest it was beating so hard!

She couldn't wait to see him again and she knew exactly where he would be this afternoon – she planned to be there also. She smiled to herself shyly as she reached the riverbank. Mick would know of her interest soon enough, and if she had her way, they would be joined at the upcoming equinox festival.

Lena regarded the river; it was so calm and peaceful here. She closed her eyes and listened to the gentle flow of the water as it meandered on to where it would eventually find the oceans. She had never seen an ocean and only knew of their existence from stories— but she believed they existed. One day she might even have a chance to see them. Well, at least she could hope.

The sun was bright this morning, warming her back as she stood there listening to the sounds of the rushing water. Opening her eyes, she looked out to the rocks jutting up from the middle of the river. She could recall many afternoons swimming to them with Hobs when they were younger. They would climb up onto them and bask in the sun while simply enjoying one another's company. Those were good times—times she hoped she would be able to remind Hobs of if she saw him again.

Setting the basket down, Lena started placing the clothes in the stone basin hewn there for washing. So intent on what she was doing, she didn't notice anything until the hand covered her mouth and a sack went over her head.

Struggle as she might Lena could not break free. Her arms were quickly bound to her sides and a gag was tied around the bag over her mouth to prevent her screaming.

A voice close to her ear hissed, "Stay quiet. Get up and walk."

Lena hesitated and was struck on the shoulder, knocking her to the ground.

"Don't hurt her."

"Why not? She's got it coming."

"That wasn't part of what we agreed to."

"Why should I care? The bitch deserves what she's going to get."

Two of them she realized as she listened to their muffled argument. Rough hands picked her up again. *Where were they taking her?* She wondered with growing fear.

"I said walk," the first voice commanded.

This time Lena did as she was told, being led quietly by her arm.

Jonaton knew he would find Abigail in the Hall of Records. He smiled as his intuition was confirmed. "Abigail," he started, "the records have been here for years, and I think you have a few more days to read all of them."

Abigail pushed her chair back and smiled up at Jonaton. "I know, I know, it's just that I find it all so interesting and exciting and..."

Jonaton's full laugh brought her thoughts back. It was an infectious laugh and one not often heard of late. Abigail liked it.

"I have much more to show you and teach you, but not here," Jonaton said, beckoning her to follow him out of the room. "Let's look at the town through the eyes of a council member. I think you will see things a bit different today from how you did before."

With that cryptic remark Abigail followed Jonaton, wondering just what he would show her.

Lena stumbled, and again the hands picked her up. She could feel the bruises forming on her legs and body where she had hit the ground over and over. The path they were taking was growing steadily uneven, and large rocks seemed to be strewn everywhere.

After what seemed like an eternity, they came to a halt.

"Hi Lena." A new voice greeted her. One that turned her blood to ice as she recognized the voice that spoke—ROLAND!

Chapter 13

As the days passed Hobs schedule intensified. From the moment he woke, Archon put him through one rigorous training program after another. Each new day was more intense than what Archon had given him prior.

Before the end of this particular morning, Hobs had a grasp of engineering basics – basics ranging over various disciplines: chemical, electrical, mechanical, and aerospace – the tests that Archon had given him to complete were thorough in evaluating both his comprehension and the practical applications of this knowledge.

Archon had completed the morning's training by uploading various astronomy and navigational programs. His grasp of both terrestrial and stellar navigation was now solid. He was able to plot courses to planets he had never heard about before today, as well as input the course plots to these planets into computers he had never used.

It was amazing all the information he could now recall and use practically. What more could Archon teach him—and what was the deep secret Archon had alluded to on multiple occasions? Why was Archon pushing him so hard?

Hobs knew he had a solid understanding of technology now but apparently Archon didn't agree with his assessment. And so the training continued as file after file was uploaded, and test after test followed.

Hobs increased his knowledge in the areas of basic and advanced medicine. This had been followed by robotics and the principles of artificial intelligence which in turn lead to long discussions about Artificial Entities – he still was vague about what an AE actually was.

It was staggering the knowledge his ancestors had once known so many years ago, knowledge that had been lost to his people as the result of the Scarian genocide. If he had anything to say about it, it was knowledge that Hobs intended to see learned once more.

Tomorrow Archon promised advance combat training; it was training that would be followed by the long promised pilot training for land, air, and spacecraft. Hobs knew enough now to actually understand what a spacecraft was and looked forward to tomorrow with anticipation.

Through the hectic schedule that Archon kept him on, he still found time to practice the piano. It was a peaceful way to relax after a long and allow his tension for flow away after a grueling day of training – while Archon appeared to find Hobs' interest in music a less important part of his training, he did his best to supply music he felt Hobs would like. While relaxing, it was also frustrating –music was much harder to master than the combat skills he was drilling in; all the same Archon said he was improving.

Archon closely watched Hobs' progress throughout the week and concluded that the boy was ready for what he had to reveal to him.

Chapter 14

Ssplin observed the activity in the hanger as the loading of the assault craft was completed – a faulty system had resulted in a repair that had delayed their launch by three days. Ssplin had been furious at the delay and his troops had been fearful around him, unsure how he would react to the delay due to his volatile nature.

That was in the past however, and now the loading was finished.

Ssplin watched as his troops moved into formation. They moved with precision and were now standing at attention waiting for his command – a command that would change his future forever and see him elevated back to his former glory. His only regret was that in order to accomplish this he had to use the rejects before him—well, it could be worse.

The craft behind them was as ugly as it was efficient. It was large enough to hold three times the troops he had. The vessel sat roughly nine meters in length and had stubby wings midway that provided stability in atmospheric maneuvers. These wings also held the ordnance that he could use to rain destruction on his enemies. On this day; however, there was only a single missile under each wing. They were all he had available to him on this godforsaken station; he could only hope they would not be needed; or if for some reason they were needed, that they would be enough. The end of the craft held the two sub-light engines. Ugly, yet efficient was his conclusion.

Turning his attention back to his troops, he regarded them with a critical eye. He paced before them, examining each of them carefully. Not exactly shock troops, but they would do. His excitement was barely contained due to the magnitude of what they were about to do. He took a deep breath before addressing his troops.

"Today will be a glorious day for Scaria; today we are embarking on a mission which will result a great victory. We will be the first Scarian to encounter our Valaran enemy in decades. Do the jobs you are ordered to do, and you will be rewarded. Fail and you will see the fruit of failure. All aboard!" he ordered.

"Yes sir," rang the combined voices of his two Hands.

He watched as his warriors swiftly boarded the craft behind their War Masters, the spring in their step proof of their excitement regarding the imminent mission. Prissng's squad was understaffed but that was how it would be. He had failed at maintaining discipline in his squad and should consider himself fortunate that he still had a head on his shoulders. With precision that indicated his training tactics were working, Ssplin watched as the troops secured harnesses and settled in for the flight.

A glance around the cabin revealed that all of their gear was properly stowed and everything was in order. With a satisfied hiss Ssplin sealed the hatch of the assault craft; he watched until the light turned green indicating a good seal and he felt the pressurization of the cabin. After a final look around the cabin, he turned and entered the cockpit where he made his way to the pilot seat. Prissng took the copilot seat beside him leaving Sszlont to take the navigator position.

"Sszlont retrieve my navigation calculations and plot a course to Cygnus Prime if you would," Ssplin ordered crisply.

Sszlont's three fingers flew over the computer. Ssplin watched him pause as he checked the results, and then proceeded to make a few changes. Satisfied with the course, he committed it to the navigational computer.

"Course entered and plotted. Destination Cygnus Prime, arrival nine days standard. Normal cryo procedures will commence immediately after takeoff," Sszlont replied with the sharpness Ssplin expected.

Ssplin's muzzle broke into the closest thing to a smile a Scarian could make; the result was truly hideous. He was content; this mission would be the crowning moment in his military career. It would be the impetus that would propel him back into the mainstream of Scarian military life. He would be exonerated!

With a push of a button Ssplin engaged the engines; the craft leapt forward, penetrating the force field protecting the landing bay with a slight resistance. The stars whirled around them as the computer initiated the course corrections required to reach their destination and then they were on their way to make history.

An hour into the flight, Ssplin watched as last of his warriors entered cyro suspension – once the flight crew was under they would accelerate to near light for the remainder of the voyage. They would be awakened six hours prior to entering the planet's atmosphere in order to allow time for the suspension drugs to be purged from their systems.

Ssplin watched both Sszlont and Prissng place the breathing masks over their muzzles before he keyed the sequence to put them both under. He quietly watched as the clamps locked over their wrists and needles were inserted that would carry the drugs into their systems; within a few short minutes they passed into the dreamless sleep of cyro suspension.

While cyro suspensions was a safe there was always a risk that you would never wake from this sleep, that you might have a lethal reaction—but they were soldiers and those thoughts were trivial and easily cast aside. He checked the monitors one after another; what he found satisfied him that all of his warriors were in proper suspension.

Ssplin would be last to go under. It was standard doctrine for the commander to be the last under the first out. He was strict in his observance of this protocol – he would take no chances that one of his War Masters or warriors would take the opportunity to put the blade to him while he slept and gain an instant promotion. A blade would end his plans fast and he was entirely too intelligent for that.

He reviewed the readings on the nav computer again and was pleased with the results. Nine days hence, they would arrive at their destination and then they would see—oh yes, they would see why Ssplin was a true military leader. He would show his father; he would show the war council; he would show them all!

He put his own mask on before he flipping the lever that would inject the chemicals and release the gases that would place him into cyro suspension. He recline back into the acceleration chair, eyes sparkling in anticipation at what was to come as the chemicals coursed through his veins inducing the artificial sleep.

The computer on the assault craft took over. All passengers were now in cryo sleep and being actively monitored. Commands were executed to protect the passengers by cocooning them in protective gelplast – this would cushion them from the effects of inertia while travelling at near light speed in the small craft.

Once that task was completed the computer accelerated the craft to its cruising speed. Barring any unforeseen accidents, they would arrive at their destination in nine days standard. In the event of an emergency, the craft would slow to a safer speed, and the Brood Warrior would be awakened to deal with the crisis.

Chapter 15

Lena cringed as they pulled her hood off. Roland stood there glaring at her; holding her up on either side were Piers and Cades as she expected. Roland was looking at her with undisguised hate in his eyes that chilled her to her core. With a sinking realization Lena knew this could only end one way, and it would not be well for her!

Roland reached up and grabbed her face under the chin. When she tried to break free from his grasp, it resulted in a vicious slap across the face.

"Bitch!" Roland said as he slapped her. "The plans you've ruined. You could have had it all, anything you wanted just by saying yes and standing by my side. Guess I wasn't good enough for you, was I? You decided to reject me; well guess what? Now you're going to pay to that."

"Cades, Piers—help me, please." Silence greeted her pleas for help as she looked from one to the other. Disgusted at their silence she turned back to Roland, "What do you want from me, Roland?"

In that moment as she looked at Roland she realized what evil truly was...

She watched Roland as he just stood there looking at her. The way his eyes roamed over her body made her sick to her stomach. He was appraising her as one would a piece of meat in his father's butcher shop. She could feel him undressing her with his eyes. The next thing she knew Roland moved directly in front of her, so close that she could feel his breath on her neck. Again she tried to pull away, and again Roland's friends just tightened their grips, holding her in place.

Roland kissed her on the neck. Not the gentle kiss of a lover, but the rough kiss of man taking what he wanted—what he thought he owned. It revolted her. She bit his tongue as he tried to kiss her on the mouth, forcing him to draw away from her.

"What's wrong, Roland, can't find a woman who wants you?" Lena taunted. "So you have to force yourself on one..."

Her taunt had a chilling effect—Roland paused for a moment. "Force?" He turned to Piers and Cades. "I think she will be begging for more by the time we are done here, won't she?" He flashed them both a wicked grin. All they could do was laugh, Cades with anticipated, Piers with trepidation.

Roland returned his gaze to Lena. Looking her in the eyes the entire time he slowly ran his hands down her sides. Pausing at her breasts, he cupped them before roughly squeezing them through her blouse. Continuing, he ran his hands down to her waist. He slowly kneeled down in front of her and paused. Lena had no clue what was coming next and didn't have to wait long to find out as Roland gripped the hem of her skirt and with a great wrench ripped it open fully up to her waist.

He stood again and looked at her with malice in his eyes. "I think you're going to like this, Lena." With that he thrust his hand between her legs and her nightmare began.

Lena stared at Roland through the pain, realizing what was coming. A quick glance to either side showed that Cades was getting excited also. Roland gave no indication that he was aware, or cared about the pain he was inflicting on her. He had lost any sense of reason and control as his excitement grew. She fought back as best she could, squirming against the two holding her.

"I think she wants more, what do you two think?" Roland asked of his friends.

"Yeah, man, go for it."

Lena was shocked to hear Cades' murmur of assent and encouragement to Roland.

Piers and Cades forced Lena to her back on the ground. Looking up, she could see Roland hastily undressing. As Roland approached her, she kicked out with all her might and kicked at him between the legs. She was unsuccessful as his friends held her down – restraining her so Roland could violate her.

"Don't do this, Roland, I beg of you."

"Maybe you shouldn't have pushed me away. Think about that, bitch."

Ignoring her further pleas, Roland violated her. All she could think of was the pain that coursed through her body and that he sounded like a rutting grazer.

Lena did her best to ignore what was happening, to pretend she was somewhere else, but all that earned her was a slap from Roland. He wanted her in the moment with him—the look of triumph in his eyes disgusted her. She spit in his face, which earned her another stinging slap in the face.

With a grunt of release he finished and rolled off of her. She felt thoroughly defiled. When she tried to get up, Cades pushed her roughly back to the ground. She glanced over to Piers, who looked like he wanted to vomit and was unsuccessfully trying to hold it back.

"That all you got, Roland? Here I thought you were a man."

Roland laughed, ignoring her retort as he put on his pants. "Who's next?"

The full weight of what was to happen hit her in that instant. They would all take turns violating her. And when they were finished, they would quite likely kill her. She fought with renewed struggles as Roland dressed quickly before slipping around to take Cades' place.

She looked into Cades' eyes. "Don't do this Cades, you can stop this. It was all Roland's fault, Jonaton will understand."

With a vicious slap that nearly knocked her senseless, she heard him bark, "Don't look at me, bitch!" He removed his shirt and pants. "Turn her over. I don't want to have her looking at me."

Lena felt pain sharper than she had with Roland as Cades violated her. She flitted on the edge of consciousness from the pain as her nightmare continued, then with a wave of nausea she passed out.

A short time later, she woke to hear Roland and Cades arguing with Piers.

"Haven't we taught her the lesson you want? I mean enough is enough already. I don't need a turn."

"You will take your turn, just like Cades and I did. You know what will happen if you don't. You know what happened to Ren." Roland concluded icily.

Shocked at what she was hearing, Lena kept her eyes closed, praying that they wouldn't notice she was awake. An unfortunate twitch gave her away.

Roland bent close to Lena's ear and said, "Are you enjoying yourself, Lena? We have one more *man* for you."

Lena opened her eyes and saw him motion Piers over. She could see the apology in his eyes as he removed his shirt, knowing what would happen to him if he didn't take his turn.

She closed her eyes, willing herself to pass out again, only to feel another vicious blow to her face. Fleetingly she wondered what her face looked like—she thought of Mick and felt disappointment that she would never be able to enter a union with him. The worst part was that he was barely aware of how she felt.

The pain was unbearable as Piers violated her. She was bruised and in pain from the prior two. This time it felt as if she was being ripped open.

Piers was the fastest of the three—almost as if to say "I'm sorry." Then he was done.

She watched him as he stood and put on his pants. Hoping against hope, she watched to see if there was any indication that they would let her go. Instead she felt Roland's foot in her side, and in that instant she knew it wouldn't be so. Cades joined in, kicking her from the other side.

As her eyes glazed over, she saw Piers turn and vomit against a tree, and then she saw no more.

Roland continued to kick and punch Lena until Cades, who had had enough, pulled him away.

"She's dead, man, enough!" Cades shouted to be heard.

Roland looked and him and laughed. "She got exactly what she deserved." With that he spat on her limp form.

Piers walked over and knelt beside her, gently touched her bloody neck – he checked for a glimmer of a pulse. It was there, faintly.

"Well?" was all Roland could ask.

In a moment Piers made his decision—he would not be a party to murder. If he had to answer for this crime, so be it! But he would not commit murder. Looking up at his friend in disgust, he lied. "She's dead."

Roland burst out into hysterical laughter. "Serves the bitch right; let's dispose of the trash."

Roland grabbed her by the legs and dragged her over to the pit that Ren had fallen into. Pausing briefly at the edge, he reflected on what they had done. *She had it coming*, he decided. All he had wanted was for her to love him, to be his mate—and she had rejected him. For what? Hobs? Anger surged through him anew as he bent down and rolled her over the edge. He watched her fall, hitting the ground below with a thud.

He didn't give Lena the dignity of burying her. Why waste his energy climbing down? After the lights in the sky, no one was coming here any time soon. She would never be found.

"I need to clean up," Roland announced to his friends. "Let's go for a swim."

With a shrill whistle he gathered the grazers and led them to the river.

Chapter 16

Alarms rang out in the control room; alarms that Archon quickly silenced. Activating his external sensors he noted that there had been another disturbance at the pit. The third such in the past few weeks only this time it was different. When he was sure that the three men had left, he dispatched two androids to retrieve the two bodies that were now there. One he carefully encased in gelplast before moving it.

He monitored their progress as the androids delivered their loads to the destination dictated in their orders. Satisfied with their progress, he proceeded to set the required automated tasks in motion.

Hobs completed his morning advanced combat training and tactics exercises. The tests that Archon had presented him with this morning were far more rigorous than any prior. He had to perform in combat these combat simulations perfectly or suffer the stinging pain that indicated he was dead.

Archon had stepped up the training to a level of intensity that required him to destroy some of Archon's combat androids; if he hadn't there was the possibility that they might have killed him.

There was no middle ground. Archon was playing this game for keeps. Hobs' reactions were almost reflex and instinct now. He was deadly on the field of combat with a solid grasp of combat tactics – he was efficient in the execution of what he was learning.

Today; however, Hobs reached the limit of his patience. After a particularly demanding simulation was complete he stormed out of the training center and returned to his room.

"ARCHON, I want answers NOW."

"Yes, Hobs, what answers do you require?" Archon's steady reply filled the room almost immediately.

"Over the past weeks I have done as you asked, learned what you wanted me to learn, and I think it is past time for you to tell me why you've done all of this," Hobs demanded.

"Very well," Archon replied, "I am dying!"

The bluntness of Archon's statement caught Hobs short. "Say what…" The shock of Archon's pronouncement caused Hobs to search through his new memories. From all the training he had received, he couldn't see how an AE could die and said so.

In answer to his question Archon continued, "In a properly maintained facility, an AE can last for many millennia. This facility, however, is in no way being properly maintained. As such my power sources have been degrading at a steady rate of decay. It is only a matter of time until they fail altogether. In the past ten years, I have lost three power plants at various facilities spread over the continent."

Archon paused, "As a result, my core has sustained irreparable damage. It is only a matter of time now before I experience full systems failure and cease to exist.

"In light of this, I have been working on a plan to place all of my knowledge and the core of who I am in protected storage, where it can last for many millennia to come. I, however, will cease to know the passing of time, and the essence of who I am will quite likely not survive the process of being stored. No AE has ever undergone this process, and the odds are not promising that any part of who I am will remain. This is partly a result of what an AE is at the core of our being." Archon paused again. "I think it would be better if I showed you something first."

The doors opened, and Hobs turned to watch an android step into his room.

"Hobs, please follow X5."

Hobs could almost hear sorrow in the AE's voice, if that was possible.

Hobs followed the android through the corridors of the facility. Deeper and deeper into the bowels of the hill they went and still they hadn't reached their destination. The corridors in this part of the facility had the appearance of not being occupied for a long time, longer than the area Hobs was kept in. Dust covered the floors, undisturbed until their passage. Just when he was sure that they could go no deeper, X5 stopped in front a door marked AE CORE.

The door whooshed opened to allow Hobs to enter a room unlike any other he had seen in the facility. His nose was assaulted by antiseptic smells, reminding him of the medical bay. Banks of machinery lined the far wall of the chamber, lights flashing as they performed their assigned tasks. In the center of the room was a large column that extended from the floor to the ceiling, wider in diameter than Hobs could wrap his arms around.

Midway up the column was a glass ring allowing the viewer to see inside the column, and what Hobs saw stopped him dead in his tracks!

Encased inside the glass was a brain suspended in a protective gel. Hundreds of leads that bore a striking resemblance to his uplink cable were attached to the brain like needles in a pincushion. With dawning realization, Hobs knew he was seeing Archon...

"Yes, Hobs," Archon broke the silence, perceiving his thoughts, "What you see is all that is left of me. This is all that remains of the Valaran I once was. A rare honor it was to be selected to the AE program and a rarer honor still to be given a facility such as this one. Little did I know of the lonely existence that was ahead of me three hundred cycles ago when the last of my technicians departed from this place...since that time I have been alone until you arrived!"

Hobs interrupted Archon with astonishment and growing fear at what he thought Archon was seeking. "You want me to take your place?" The thought was more than he could comprehend in spite of his new knowledge. He could almost hear a laugh in Archon's reply.

"No, Hobs, we do not have the ability to do what you suggest. Had you been listening, you would also remember that this facility is also dying, not just me. This place has existed for over a millennium. That is much longer than the designers had intended without maintenance and upgrades. It will soon cease to exist. The steady decay of this facility and its system have resulted in damage to my core. It is now only a matter of time until I cease to exist," Archon stated as a simple matter of fact.

This response left Hobs perplexed. "Then what is it that you want of me?"

Archon answered slowly, "Before you arrived, I had resigned myself to the inevitability of existence as nothing more than a memory, a shadow, a dim recollection. But you have brought me hope!

"You have the potential to be my salvation, Hobs. You are a true Valaran, maybe even one of the last remaining. You have returned to me in my time of crisis and greatest need."

What Archon said hit Hobs like a ton of stones. VALARAN!

"WHAT!" Hobs blurted out. "I am no more Valaran than you are human. Well, you were human, but...oh DAMN IT, you know what I mean, I am NOT Valaran."

"Your denial doesn't make it any less of the truth that it is, young Hobs. Your physical appearance shouts your heritage from your jet-black hair to your dark blue eyes with their flecks of red. If that wasn't enough, the tests I ran on your blood confirmed it. Your DNA declares you to be Valaran, and not just a descendant of Valara—your blood is almost pure. I have not been able to ascertain how, but your parents had to both be Valaran. The Scarian failed in their attempt to exterminate our race," Archon stated with a note of triumph.

"If that isn't enough, the manner in which your body integrated the implants also confirms what I am telling you. The spinal implant has only ever been successfully integrated with Valaran physiology. The process is less successful with other races. Where it was been tried, some motor skills were recovered, but never the full range of motion that the recipient had prior to the accident. Yet it worked on you! Look at you, walking, fighting—doing things that weeks ago you may never have had the chance to do due to the extent of your injuries."

"So," Hobs decided to try again, "what does this have to do with me? What is it you want, if not to replace you here?"

"I propose a partnership!" was Archon's stunning reply.

When Hobs didn't answer, Archon continued. "I could not have predicted this possibility in all of my probability calculations, but here we are. I placed within you a processing node capable of storing my essence. If the transfer is successful, I would be able to communicate with you sub vocally, and aid you in accessing the untapped areas of your mind. I could help you with reaction times and responses in ways we cannot even imagine at this time. As I said, a partnership! An **amalgam** if you will—a synthesis of man and AE."

"Why didn't you just do this while I was unconscious?" Hobs asked. "I mean, why go through all of this training and what not?"

"It is simple," Archon stated. "You are Valaran, the maker. I could not violate you in such a manner as to do what I propose without your agreement. I need you to want this partnership. If you choose not to enter into it then I will simple fade into obscurity, a memory. I want to live, Hobs!"

The earnestness of the plea struck Hobs as he gazed at the column. "You make a compelling argument, but I need time to consider it," he answered.

"Time is something we do not have in great quantity," was Archon's response.

"What do you mean?"

"Only that a transmission was discovered being sent from a Scarian satellite in orbit. The contents of the message indicated the discovery of this facility. It is only a matter of time until the Scarian arrive to investigate. If they follow their past history, they will arrive in numbers great enough to exterminate all life on this planet," Archon stated in a deadpan tone as if he was giving the time of day.

The silence was thundering as Archon concluded his pronouncement. Hobs knew there was only one logical thing he could do...

"I agree to our partnership, Archon; however, I must insist on one condition..." Hobs paused. "I will always retain full control of my body and mind. You will be a silent partner assisting me."

"Assent," was all Archon replied.

Hobs turned and exited the room; once in the corridor he indicated to X5 to lead him back to his quarters.

Chapter 17

Abigail and Jonaton had spent the day touring the community. He had shown her many things and had opened her eyes to what the council actually did. To think, people thought they only mediated disagreements and presided over the equinox. She was awestruck at how the council actually subtly guided the community. They directed projects from behind the scenes, projects that only made the community better.

The farmlands project south of town was one such endeavor – Abigail looked out in awe as they stood on a bluff overlooking the farms.

"All this took eight years to prepare?"

"There were quite a few skills to learn. Ren had to be able to make the piping that we used to deliver water to the fields, a suitable location had to be found, and the right people prepared."

"Eight years though. So let's see if I understand this correctly. You built a water wheel on higher ground beside the river. It collects water in buckets, emptying them into a cistern. These pipes Ren fabricated allow the water to flow out of the bottom of the cistern, through the pipes, ending at this field. The farmers can then move these 'sprinklers' where they are needed because of this flexible, what did you call it, hose?" The sprinklers were long pipes on massive wheels. Small holes in the bottom of the pipe allowed water to flow to the ground where needed.

"See, you understand. Once the other farmers saw how it worked, they all wanted access to the irrigation system."

"And all of the designs came from these documents you mentioned."

"Yes."

"And you have no idea where the documents came from?" Abigail asked incredulously.

"We have no idea where the older documents came from; however, Parem brought a sheaf new ones when he and Rowena arrived in town. The paper is the same, so we can only guess they knew the source – unfortunately I was never able to find out before they passed."

"So over the years, the council would simply choose a project from the documents and make it a reality."

"In simple terms, yes. You must realize that most of these plans will take years to implement, and people have to be willing to learn new skills."

"So let me guess, this is why you are such a staunch defender of education?"

"Exactly, my dear."

"And Pol doesn't know about these documents."

"Pol wouldn't be able to grasp their significance even if he was aware of them. Pol is only interested in what benefits himself, not others. As Historian, you need to know. It is now your responsibility to protect these documents for the future. I decided to champion the farmlands expansion. That took time, but look at the results. We can now sustain ourselves and have additional food to trade for things we need. I followed with fertilization, and Ren chose to introduce irrigation."

She chuckled as she regarded Jonaton. "Well, at least *you* found another use for grazers. And how you managed your breeding program is beyond belief. To think, people had no clue they were being carefully guided in regards to who to mate with."

"I can't stress how important that aspect of the plan is, Abigail. Without it we would not have been able to prevent the birth defects that had been rampant in prior years before the program. The goal is to keep the population healthy and thriving. We send young men and women from our community to the three nearest towns under the pretext of apprenticing. We then apprentice suitable men and women from those towns here in Redwood. Everything is done in the hope that these young people will fall in love and enter into the union with a local man or women. The end result is the gradual expanding and strengthening of our bloodlines. There were a handful of families that resisted this process. I bet you can guess one of them."

"Pol's?"

"Got it in one! The reason his family was brought into the council was in the hope that they would see past their parochialism and realize the greater good the council was working towards. That plan failed miserably! This failure would have continued if not for Roland's actions. Pol had won a victory by stonewalling the irrigation project, one that was vitally necessary if the farmlands project was to succeed—Pol's price had been Roland's future on the council. Roland, by his own actions, has removed that future from ever having the possibility to see its fruition. Pol is a council mistake of the greatest magnitude. He doesn't believe in or support the 'plan' unless there is something in it for him, as a result we have to proceed with care."

"I think I see why Pol was so furious with Roland after the judgment. There's more though, isn't there, Jonaton?"

"Yes there is. You need to know that I have been gently guiding Lena to Mick. The match is a good one since he is the result of the union of a woman his father met while apprenticing in the town of Elder Creek. Lena appears truly interested in Mick. Unfortunately, Mick is the one I'm not quite sure about."

"But what about Hobs, where does he fit in all of this?"

"Hobs is a wildcard. Both of his parents were unique, and any union he made would expand the bloodlines—including one with Lena if they both chose it."

"Wow. I never realized all of this was happening in our town—and even more amazing that councils from other towns are cooperating with one another. It will take some getting used to, but you have my full support, even where it touches Lena."

"That is refreshing to hear Abigail. Shall we return to town? There is more I'd like to show you."

Jonaton lit the lamp in the Hall of Records before moving to the only part of the wall not lined with bookshelves. Abigail watched as he moved a piece of trim, exposing a keyhole into which he inserted a small silver key. With a click, she watched as the cleverly hidden door swung open, exposing a small cubby inside.

Peering into the cubby, the only thing she saw was a stack of pages, which Jonaton carefully removed. Fearing that the ancient pages would crumble as he moved them, she scrutinized his every move until they were safely on the table.

She breathed a sigh of awe. "Ooo, look at these pages. How old are they? What ink did they use? I can't believe that there isn't any fading or signs of aging. What makes the letters stand out like that?"

"Amazing, isn't it," she heard Jonaton reverently whisper, interrupting her rambling.

"I have never seen anything like these," she replied with a soft chuckle. "Who else knows about them?"

"Ren was the only other current council member who knew of them. I never trusted Pol enough to make him privy to this great secret."

"May I?" she asked, indicating the pages.

With great care, Abigail picked up the top sheet from the stack.

"Look, this outlines the details of the farmlands project you just showed me." Shuffling through the next few pages, she said, "And the irrigation plan just as you described it."

Jonaton took the top page and handed it to Abigail to examine in more detail. "As you can see on that page, every project has a brief explanation of the merits of the project in simple terms, plus skills that we would have to 'learn'. The 'creator' of these documents realized we would have to work and learn to be able to implement these projects."

Abigail set the pages aside and proceeded to browse over a few more pages. She paused on the page outlining the bloodlines project. It was exactly as Jonaton had described it, again with the simple explanation on the top of the first page regarding why it was important.

"I think these pages, even more than your explanations, help me understand why past councils chose to implement these projects slowly. If they had tried to implement all of these projects at once, they would have overwhelmed the people."

"I think you also understand why we have had to keep this information a secret also then."

"Oh I do, Jonaton, I do."

Still flipping through the projects, one page struck Abigail as a perfect idea. Removing it from the stack, she turned to Jonaton and said, "I want to work on this project by your permission."

Jonaton took the papers and read them carefully. Abigail watched the smile slowly spread on Jonaton's face as he read.

"I think this is perfect at this time, Abigail my dear. It will take a lot of work in order to accomplish this project—it will keep you quite busy," Jonaton concluded, "but if anyone can make this happen, I think that person is you."

Collecting the pages, he replaced them on the top of the stack. Then with the same care he had shown removing them, he returned them to the cubby, carefully locking it. He made sure that the molding covered the keyhole properly before stepping away.

Turning to Abigail he said, "I think that our agreement on your proposed project is all we need on this matter. I see no reason to include Pol."

Abigail nodded in assent.

"The printing press—who would have thought you would have selected that project, yet it is so appropriate."

Pleased that she had chosen well, Abigail started to follow Jonaton from the Hall of Records. He paused at the door before turning to her. With a flourish and a bow, he handed her the small silver key and said, "You are now the hope of our future. I am passing to you the mantle of leadership."

"Me...but I've just joined the council."

"Exactly you! I am getting old, Abigail, and I must see that the future of the council is in the hands of competent leadership. I have chosen you."

"I don't know what to say except thank you. I will work hard to prove your faith in me."

"I have no doubt you will, Abigail, no doubt at all. Shall we go?"

After closing the door to the Hall of Records, he paused at the desk and took three pages from his tunic. He handed one to her, kept one and put the final copy back in the desk.

Opening the document with trembling hands, she noted that it was the formal transfer of council leadership to her. She thought about how angry Pol would be when he found out, a thought that lasted no more than a second before turning to one of ecstasy.

Leaving the council hall, Abigail and Jonaton headed toward Pol's house. Knocking loudly, they waited for him to open the door a moment later.

"Jonaton. Abigail. To what do I owe this visit?"

"Just a small matter of council business Pol; it should only take a minute of your time." Handing Pol a copy of the document Jonaton continued, "This is a formal transfer of leadership from me to Abigail..."

"WHAT?"

"Just a matter of formality, nothing to..."

"You can't do this—I have seniority on the council. Leadership should transfer to me."

"Seniority is not required when selecting my replacement. I have full rights to transfer my position to whomever I wish. Precedent is quite clear in the records—you might know this if you spent a bit more time reviewing them."

"I will fight this decision, old man."

"You can TRY and fight it Pol, but unless you can prove me incompetent—and you can't—Abigail is the new leader of council and as such you will respect her and support her decisions as you have mine."

"We'll see about that." Pol slammed his door closed in their faces.

"That could have gone smoother," Abigail said, turning to Jonaton. "I actually thought he might strike you there."

"For a minute I thought he might also." Jonaton led the way to his house. "When all is said and done though, there isn't a thing Pol can do about it. The decision is mine and mine alone to make."

"Oh I agree, I've read enough in the records and council rules to know that you are well within your rights to select your successor. I also know that unless there is sufficient proof that you are incapable of making a rational decision then your decision isn't subject to a vote."

"Exactly my dear, and since Pol doesn't have any such proof, my decision is final."

As they reached Jonaton's house Abigail spoke up. "I hope you don't mind, I asked Lena to tidy up for you—she may still be here."

Jonaton waved that off, saying, "That's fine. It's kind of you to look after me the way you do."

Opening the door to his house, it only took a moment for them both to reach the same conclusion.

Jonaton seemed a bit puzzled. "I don't think Lena's been here."

"I wonder what could have kept her?" Abigail questioned, looking up at the sun to determine the time. "She should have been here hours ago."

With that comment, Abigail rushed out the door and ran to her house, where she threw open the door. Lena wasn't there either! Looking quickly around her, she noted that the laundry basket was missing. Could Lena still be at the river?

She barely heard Jonaton shouting for her to wait as she ran from the town to the river—branches snapped at her and she blindly ran down the path through the forest. She burst out onto the grasslands and ran down to the waters edge. She pulled up short; there on the bank of the river by the washbasin was the laundry basket. Running over to it, she saw the clothes in the basin still unwashed. On the ground she saw many footprints and what appeared to be the marks of something being dragged.

She was brought short by laughing voices coming from upstream; laughter that was followed by the bleating of grazers. Roland, she thought icily.

Moments later they came into view just as Jonaton and a band of men arrived from town.

Jonaton stepped in front of Abigail as she moved to confront the three young men. "Calm yourself, Abigail," he whispered, "let me handle this."

He looked at the washbasin and the basket beside it with the dirty clothing it still contained. Then he looked at the young men with their clothes still wet from their swim. He noted the signs of struggle on the ground around the basin, and with a sinking realization he knew with a sickening certainty what must have happened, yet he also knew they would not be able to prove it.

"Roland, Piers, Cades…" he said, making sure he had their attention before continuing. "Lena appears to be missing. Have you seen her?"

He could sense some nervousness in Roland for a brief moment before he answered calmly, "No sir, we were with the grazers all day. I took them to the north pastures, but we decided on a quick swim on the way back to remove the grazer stench."

"That is strange because from the signs it appears as if there was a struggle here, so I would say she disappeared from this spot, plus her laundry is still here."

"Well, we haven't seen her. It might be possible to organize a search, but I'm not sure how much ground you could cover with the light fading as fast as it is."

Looking at the three boys, Jonaton made a decision—motioning to one of the men from town, he told him to take the grazers to town. He turned to the boys and said, "You three will help search for Lena."

"Like hell I will," Roland replied, storming back to town.

Piers and Cades almost followed him but a single scorching stare from Jonaton made them think better of it.

Addressing those gathered, he issued orders to start a search for Lena, fanning out from the washbasin. He made it clear that Piers and Cades were not to follow the path of struggle unless the group determined that was the only path to follow.

He then led the stricken Abigail back to his house, where he did his best to comfort her as she cried out over and over, "Lena," weeping the entire time.

Two hours later, Jonaton opened the door and took the report from the search parties.

"I am so sorry, Jonaton. We lost Lena's trail. All signs of the struggle ended in the rocky terrain just northeast of the river; because it was so dark we couldn't follow the trail any further."

"We can start again in the morning, maybe…"

The hunter interrupted him, "There's more, Jonaton. Howler calls were heard to the northeast. I'm not sure how many people are going to be willing to search for her when there are howlers prowling about."

"I understand. We will just have to make sure the search teams are large and well equipped. Thank you for trying. Go home and rest, we can pick this up in the morning."

Closing the door, he turned and looked at Abigail. He had finally gotten her to fall asleep—with a groan he wondered what he would tell her in the morning.

Chapter 18

Hobs was lost in the facility – his mind a swirling maelstrom from the revelation Archon had given him.

The android was so slow that Hobs had left him behind in frustration and was proceeding on his own. It hadn't taken long until he was totally turned around—with no clue where to go; he wasn't about to ask Archon for help yet so he had to find a terminal…

His head was reeling. He knew he could say no, but should he? Archon had saved his life. Who was he to not do the same for Archon? All of the knowledge he was receiving was opening a wealth of new horizons for him; ones that he had never known existed a few weeks ago.

How would he be able to go back to the simple life of a grazer tender, or even a metal smith?

The things he could show Ren on how to improve the metal workings—for that matter the things he could do for the town itself.

If he didn't find a terminal soon, he would have to admit defeat and ask Archon for help, but he wasn't ready for that – he wanted more time to think; time to consider the ramifications of what Archon was asking.

Passing an open door, Hobs was brought to an abrupt halt. He took an inadvertent step back, as he looked into the room shock filled his face.

NO! It couldn't be…

Slowly he entered the room and fell to the floor with a wail. "REN!"

Hobs knew without a doubt that his father was dead. The bruising was hideous and the smell of decay heavy in the room. What could have happened? How did he get to this place?

He was so deep in his grief that Hobs didn't hear Archon gently addressing him at first. "HOBS?"

"Archon, what happened to him? What happened to my father?"

"Hobs, please understand that this facility no longer has the full range of visual sensors that I had in the past. He was found at the same entrance to this facility at which you were found. I monitored the presence of two individuals. After a brief discussion, one seemed to push the other into the pit. This is the person who fell. Shortly after, two other individuals appeared and helped to lower the one who had pushed your father down into the pit to check on him. When they concluded that he was dead, they covered him with rocks and left."

Archon's narrative of the events was succinct, but it was also enough to turn Hobs' heart hard with fury—Roland!

"Hobs," Archon continued. "There is one more thing I require your assistance with… Please follow X11 to the medical unit." X11 appeared at the door at the conclusion of Archon's words.

"No, I want to stay here."

"Hobs, there is nothing you can do for your father, and I assure you that what I need to show you is critical, and YOU can help with this."

"What is it, Archon?"

"Hobs, it would be better if you went to see for yourself."

Silently Hobs followed the android from the room, pausing for a quick question. "Will you bury my father?" he asked Archon.

"With all the honors of a noble leader," was Archon's reply.

Hobs turned and didn't look back.

The android led Hobs down three corridors to the medical unit. He knew where he was when the antiseptic smells assaulted his nose. The fact that the door didn't open at his approach caused Hobs to wonder why.

"Hobs, the person in this room was also found in the pit. She had been discarded there, presumably left for dead. She was in fact near death when I retrieved her…" Archon paused. "I fear there may be some instability as a result of what was inflicted upon her, that is why I asked for you to be here. It might be helpful for her to see a human face when she wakes. It could aid in the restoration of her equilibrium as she recovers."

With that the door swooshed open, and Hobs felt as if he had been punched in the gut...

LENA!

"God no! How can this be, Archon? What happened to her?"

He rushed to her side, careful not to touch her broken body as he examined her. With care he brushed aside her hair and looked at the massive bruises on her beautiful face. He gently shook her shoulder, attempting to wake her without success.

"Why won't she wake?" he pleaded of Archon.

"I had her sedated while we worked on repairing her body. The bones have been mended and I have done everything possible for the internal injuries. The bruising will start fade within a few days, but the mental scars will take much longer. I have done all I can; now she will need your strength to continue the healing process."

"But what happened to her? How did she get beaten like this?"

"She appears to have been raped and then beaten by three individuals. The same individuals who were involved with what befell your father," Archon stated as if it was a simple matter of fact.

The fury within Hobs intensified. "Wake her," was all he could say.

She was climbing out from a deep, dark hole—grasping for a light that was eluding her; at least that was how Lena felt. Things in the dark were reaching for her, dragging her down, trying to keep her from reaching the light. The pain was so intense; she felt like surrendering to the pain, to give in to the creatures in the dark, but something – no some one, kept calling to her. It was a voice she felt that she should know, but try as she could, she couldn't identify.

The vivid nightmare expanded and she started to identify smells. They were bitter smells that assaulted her senses, and she didn't like it. With a scream she sat up and opened her eyes.

"HOBS!"

She must be dreaming. It was Hobs, yet it wasn't...his was the voice that had been calling to her in her nightmare.

She wildly looked around without recognition of where she was—everything was strange and alien except for Hobs. "Where am I?" What is this place?"

She turned to him again, and she noted that he didn't seem out of place in the room. "Hobs." With a surge of emotion she fell into his arms, weeping into his strong shoulders. She felt his arms tighten around her, comforting her.

"Lena, Lena, Lena." He held her tenderly.

She cried for what seemed like hours until everything came back in a rush—Roland, Cades, and Piers!

She pushed away from Hobs and huddled into a ball as tightly into the corner as she could. She felt like she would be sick as she remembered what had happened to her. The last thing she could recall hearing had been Roland asking if she was dead, and Piers responding yes. But she hadn't been, Piers had lied to Roland—and then she was falling; after that everything went black, only to wake up here with Hobs.

One thing made its way through her confused mind—Hobs wouldn't hurt her, he had never hurt her. She turned to Hobs and saw the depth of his concern peering back at her. Hobs had always been a rock, a true friend, and she needed his strength now.

"It is you, isn't it?" Her voice trembled and tears flowed freely down her face.

"Yes, Lena, it's me."

"But you were lost. Everyone was saying you had to be dead."

"I assure you I am not dead, Lena, in fact I don't think I have ever been more alive."

"Where's Roland and Cades—oh and Piers didn't want to, but they forced him to..."

She burst into uncontrollable sobs and shaking; Hobs drew her into an embrace and comforted her. In a matter of minutes she fell back to sleep. She was safe now for the time being; Hobs was here, everything was okay. She was unaware of the sedative that Archon had added to her IV that allowed her to sleep.

"Hobs, I have prepared the room next to yours. She will heal in body, but your companionship will now be required to heal her mind. For now she will sleep. I introduced a mild sedative to calm her once she returned to you. I am confident that the healing process had begun for her mind."

Without a word, Hobs gently picked her up and carried her through the corridors following X11.

He laid her gently on the bed Archon had prepared. He covered her with a light blanket before leaning over to brush a loose strand of hair from her face. His poor Lena, he thought, not that she was his, and now that he thought on it, she might never be his Lena. He realized that his care for her was more how one would treat his little sister. With cold fury he realized he would make Roland and his friends pay for what they had done...

He left her room, listening as the door whoosh quietly closed behind him – with grim determination he strode across the training facility. He had only been in the armory once, and that was before his training had intensified. His fury unleashed as he slammed his palm against the doorplate, entering the armory with a single purpose...

He reviewed the manifest by the door, locating the items that he required. He passed shelf after shelf unexamined as he made his way to where the combat suits were stored.

The combat suit was constructed from a lightweight bodysuit containing a network of micro generators that when activated formed a protective energy field around the wearer. This force field would protect the wearer with what amounted to light body armor—it could turn a blade and even stop small arms fire—but it was limited in its duration. If you took enough damage it would overload the system.

Hobs looked at the various colors and patterns, and settled on black—black to match his mood!

After stripping, he putting the combat suit on, noting that the fit was perfect. He could feel the suit integrated with the neural filaments in his body – he was surprised that Archon had failed to mention that phenomenon in all of his training. Maybe Archon didn't know it would occur.

Testing the neural interface, he activated the body armor with a simple thought, PROTECT. The force field hummed to life; microfilaments from the collar extended to provide protection for his head. With another command he turned the field off.

Satisfied, he moved to the utility belts and selected one that served his purpose. He fastened it around his waist and removed a few of the survival items that would not be required and replaced them instead with a micro scanner, medical scanner, and a tracking unit.

In the next rack he selected a blaster, small yet lethal. He had trained with one quite successfully, his scores at the marksman level. Hefting the weapon, he noted its weight and balance. It felt good in his hand. He would, however, have to change the holster. It required a search of a few minutes before he found one appropriate for a left-handed person. After holstering the blaster he clipped it to the belt. Next, he grabbed a few extra power cells for the weapon adding them to the utility belt.

One final thing—while a blaster was good, he still liked the Kal'Tel as his favorite weapon! He had worked with it every day since he started training and decided that he wanted one with him. He moved to the far side of the room where the swords were stored. He examined on blade after another, finding fault with each one. He passed over ones that were obviously newer before settling on one with a well-worn grip, years of use evident. He pulled the blade from its scabbard and examined it carefully. It was a superb weapon, much finer than what he had practiced with, and the balance was perfect. It was obvious to Hobs that a master had used and cared for this weapon.

This weapon wasn't just for close combat, and his training had been very thorough. He knew that with his augmented reflexes, he would be able to deflect small blaster fire if necessary.

He held the Kal'Tel before him in a formal salute and activated the energy field. The weapon sparked with life, giving the appearance of a blue fire shimmering on the length of the blade. Satisfied, he deactivated the weapon and returned it to its sheath. In a fluid motion he strapped it onto his back.

Smiling grimly to himself, Hobs knew he was ready!

Archon watched as Hobs progressed through the armory, noting each selection he made. He quietly sent instructions to add these items as well as others to the assault craft he was preparing. Hobs and he would need a way to get off the planet if required, and Archon believed in being prepared.

He was concerned, however, that Hobs was being irrational and about to launch a vendetta. "Hobs?" The voice of Archon broke the silence. "What do you think you are doing?"

"Doing?" was Hobs angry response. "Doing? I am going to avenge my father and Lena—that's what I'm going to do."

"You are not ready to leave, Hobs," Archon replied, watching him storm from the armory. "Besides, Lena NEEDS you here."

That comment stopped Hobs in his tracks. Archon was correct as usual; he would stay until Lena was ready to go home, then…

Hobs thought about what he would do then with cold, methodical planning. Yes, he would avenge his father and Lena.

"You win, for now!" he concluded, his anger cooled slightly as he headed to his room to eat – cooled, but it wasn't gone. There would be a reckoning to pay.

Lena woke hungry, wondering where she was. Fear threatening to overwhelm her as she thought about what had happened to her. With extreme effort she pushed those memories and fears aside and sat up in the bed. Her body ached all over; she knew it hadn't been a dream. She looked around the room in confusion, while not as strange as the room that she woke in before, it still wasn't Redwood—where was she, better yet where was Hobs?

Determined to find him, she looked around for her clothes but they were nowhere to be found. Instead, there was some unusual clothing draped over a chair beside a table – the only other furniture in the room. She could only assume they had been left for her. On the table itself was a funny device, but try as she might, she couldn't determine what it was for. Ignoring it for the time being, she moved to the chair, picked up the clothes, and put them on. The fit was perfect.

The whoosh of the opening door startled her yet no one entered; instead she could hear sounds of exertion coming from the other room. She moved to the door and stopped, perplexed by what she saw.

Hobs was working through intricate movements with a peculiar-looking weapon. His movements were fluid, like he was performing a dance. She watched in disbelief as Hobs completed the dance of the blade with precision. She had never seen him like this before; something had changed. The difference was something that would have caused her to fear him if he hadn't been her friend.

When he finished, he noticed her standing there and flashed her a timid smile. She watched as he sheathed the weapon in the scabbard strapped to his back. Then he turned and walked toward her.

He was different, his appearance, the way he held himself. If she didn't know him so well, she would be deathly afraid at this moment.

"Are you hungry?" Hobs asked gently.

Lena nodded her head.

Hobs smiled at her and led her back into her room. "This will take some getting used to, I imagine. It was all so new to me at first. This device here," he pointed to what looked like a box in the wall, "is where we can get food."

She watched as he removed some plates from the recess he had pointed to – what he held smelled divine.

Hobs motioned her over to the table, and the two of them proceeded to eat a dinner such as she had never eaten before. As they ate, Hobs told her some of what had happened with him. It was the most pleasant evening Lena had been part of for a long time and helped to sooth her mind from what had happened to her. Whenever the memories threatened to overwhelm her she would focus on Hobs and what he was telling her.

She didn't remember falling asleep, or Hobs carrying her to her bed and gently kissing her good night as he covered her with the light blanket. For Lena all was well in this one moment – she felt safe…for now.

"You have to stop doing that, Archon."

"Sleep is essential for Lena at this time. Her body is still healing from the trauma."

"Well at least warn me next time. I almost didn't catch her there."

"I knew you would not let her fall, Hobs. Now shall we return to your training?"

Chapter 19

At an hour before sunrise, the indicator Archon had been waiting for started blinking. The upload to the storage facility was complete. A "backup" of his core, as well as a complete backup of the databanks, was safely stored.

There was one last thing to prepare—the final upload for Hobs' training. With great care in the selection, Archon added additional packets to the upload. He planned to store as many useful programs as he deemed necessary into Hobs' long-term memory. They would be stored as deep as Archon could place them so that he would be able to access them when required yet they would not accessible to Hobs – Archon had no desire to overwhelm him with the amount of data he was going to transfer.

Today they would continue the piloting training that had been interrupted by Lena's arrival. Hobs was proving to be an excellent pilot; his skills were bordering on intuitive as he worked through the simulators.

They had completed his Advanced Combat Training program the day before. Last-minute changes had been made based on Hobs' reaction to what had happened to Lena.

Five days is what Archon estimated it would take for Hobs to work through all the flight simulations. Hopefully, they would have enough time.

When morning came, Archon was finished with everything but the final package that would transfer his "consciousness" as well as the data package. He was ready!

Hobs anger was still evident; he needed to learn some self-control or he would succeed in getting himself killed. Archon decided it would be expedient to work off Hobs' remaining anger with a set of fast-paced simulations.

A stirring in Lena's room prompted Archon to activate chimes that would awaken Hobs.

"What?" was Hobs' groggy answer.

"Lena is waking, and it would be expeditious if you were there to have breakfast with her," Archon answered.

Archon watched as Hobs rose. He put on his shipsuit, fastened the belt and blaster around his waist. Then as an afterthought, he strapped the Kal'Tel on his back and exited his room.

Lena was just dressing when the chimes to her room announced a visitor.

"Come in." She was happy this morning—something about this place made her feel safe, plus Hobs was near. Here, she felt removed from the nightmares haunting her dreams. She had waken in the middle of the night in a cold sweat, but after realizing where she was and that Hobs was near and that he would protect her, she had drifted off again and slept until morning.

"Good morning, Lena," Hobs said as he entered the room. "Hungry?"

"Starving!" Lena replied, sitting on the edge of her bed. She was troubled by the weapons so obviously displayed; she knew that Hobs was furious with Roland for what he had done—she only hoped he didn't do anything stupid.

She watched as Hobs walked over to the dispenser and ordered breakfast for the two of them. Following him with her eyes, she watched as he sat at the desk waiting for their food. Hesitation was obvious in Hobs' eyes as he sat there – he had something to say but appeared to not know how to say it. So Lena sat and waited patiently.

"Lena," Hobs began after collecting his thoughts, "there is someone I need to introduce you to, but I don't want you to be afraid. Remember what I told you last night, about the things that had happened to me?"

Lena nodded yes, so Hobs continued. "Well, this facility is run by Archon...and um," he paused, still perplexed about how to go on, "Archon takes a bit getting used to, and well...might be a bit frightening at first until you get to know him—so just accept it when I say don't try to understand what Archon is."

Lena wasn't sure what Hobs was trying to say to her, so she just sat there confused... "Okay," she said with a forced smile. He was starting to scare her a bit. Who or what was this Archon he kept mentioning?

"Archon, please say hi to Lena."

Lena watched Hobs say this out loud as if addressing the room itself. She began to wonder if Hobs had hit his head too hard when he had fallen...

Lena's mouth dropped open when a voice replied, "It is a pleasure to make your acquaintance, young Lena. Welcome to my facility. I trust you are feeling well this morning?"

"Fine thank you," Lena managed to stutter in reply, looking around her in confusion at the words that she had heard.

"Your breakfast will soon be ready, I hope you enjoy it." Continuing, Archon informed Hobs, "we have Combat and Flight training when you have finished Hobs. If you wish, Lena can observe from the command center."

"I'm not sure about training today, Archon," Hobs replied. He had things to prepare for, and that didn't include time for training.

"Oh but I am," Archon interrupted. "It will allow you to excise some of your anger, plus you will need the skills in the days ahead."

"As you wish, Archon," Hobs conceded in frustration.

Any additional conversation was interrupted by the chime of the food dispenser indicating the arrival of their breakfast. Hobs gathered the dishes and he and Lena enjoyed the hot meal while keeping each other company. All the time, Hobs' thoughts focused on Roland and how he would pay for what he had done...

The combat training that Archon had prepared for him was intense to put it lightly. It wasn't so subtle a change in the combat simulations either. One after another the simulations pitted him against the bipedal reptilian race of the Scarian—the race that had annihilated his and Archon's ancestors. They were lethal in their intensity, and a single mistake could cost Hobs. He had to put his plans for revenge out of his mind and focus on the task at hand. It was the exact result Archon had intended. By the time he was finished, Hobs was drenched in sweat, but had a firm grasp of Scarian battle tactics as well as their command structure.

The Scarian society itself was governed by a War Council. Everything in their society was geared toward keeping the war machine alive and functioning. Their young were indoctrinated at an early age in the traditions of war, perpetuating the cycle of violence that marked their civilization. Those not worthy of a place in the war machine were relegated to the menial tasks required to keep the machine alive. It was a brutal culture.

The War Council appointed Prefects to oversee the armies. These armies were divided into legions. Brood Commanders were the commanding officers over a legion. They reported directly to the Prefect assigned to that legion. Each Prefect had the command of five legions. Under the Brood Commanders were Brood Warriors. Each Brood Commander had twenty Brood Warriors reporting to them with various areas of responsibility.

The Brood Warrior commanded up to ten Hands. A Hand was comprised of a War Master and four troopers. Archon had shown Hobs recordings of how effective the Hand could be, and how disciplined they were. Hobs had been duly impressed. The Scarian were both ruthless and relentless—a fierce opponent to say the least.

If Archon was correct, and he likely was, the Scarian would shortly invade his home. That would only be trouble!

How many legions would the Scarian dispatch? What would happen to his friends and the towns surrounding Redwood? These and many other questions flooded Hobs' mind, shunting all other considerations aside.

Lena gripped the arms of her chair tighter.

"I feel like I am moving with him." The motion of the craft Hobs was piloting was giving her a sick feeling in her stomach. She swallowed against the rising nausea, feeling as if she was going up and down in a roiling motion.

"It is only an illusion, young Lena. I can dampen the effect if you wish."

"I'll be all right; thanks though."

"There is something you would like to know, isn't there?"

"Hobs and I grew up together. I am confused—how he can know all...this?"

"The explanation would be beyond your ability to understand, Lena. Suffice it to say that he has the ability to learn swiftly due to his unique heritage as a Valaran." It was a lie, but one with a grain of truth.

Lena laughed. "I think you're right, I don't understand. Archon?"

"Yes, Lena."

"Thank you for taking care of Hobs. It pleases me to see him happy like this."

"You are welcome young Lena."

She spent the rest of the morning watching as Hobs piloted various land vehicles one after another. This was followed by a selection of watercrafts. It was a wonder to her, all these amazing things she was seeing. How could it all exist?

After a quick lunch, Archon took Hobs through various aircraft simulations—that was when the real nausea started. All the twists, turns, and rolls Hobs took at high speeds. Lena had no clue how Hobs was able to manage it.

Archon was not holding back either. He had a variety of air combat simulations prepared for Hobs. He needed to see how Hobs would handle them. As far as Lena could tell, he did quite well!

"Umm, Archon?"

"Yes."

"You can help me with the nausea now if you want."

"As you wish." The arrival of the android was so prompt that Lena was sure Archon had anticipated her need. Not that she minded, since the drink it provided stopped the nausea almost immediately.

With that settled, Lena continued to watch in wonder as Hobs flew among the stars. The stars!

"Hobs demonstrates a natural skill for piloting, wouldn't you say?"

"Yes, he does." Lena didn't understand everything Archon was saying, so she listened quietly to his explanations, commenting where she felt it was appropriate.

Hobs pushed away from the table; they had enjoyed another pleasant meal together yet he was still wound tight from the rigorous workouts Archon had subjected him too. "I need to unwind; would you like to hear me play some music?"

"You!" Lena replied incredulously. "You can barely put two notes together."

"Ya, well about that. I think you might be in for a pleasant surprise."

"This I have to hear. Lead on," Lena rose and gestured to the door.

Hobs smiled as he led the way to the music hall. He was satisfied to hear the gasp of awe that she made when she entered the hall – the sound of her voice echoed through the room. He led her to the piano and sat her beside him – rifling through the music he kept on hand he found a soothing sonnet that he liked to play.

Focus, he told himself mentally. *No mistakes.*

He wanted the music to be perfect for Lena. After taking a deep, calming breath he launched into the sonnet and while not perfect, he was able to play the song with hardly any mistakes.

As the last note faded he turned to Lena.

"That was beautiful Hobs." She stated as a tear trickled down her cheek, "thank you for sharing that with me. Can you play another?"

"Of course."

He spent the next two hours playing one song after another for her.

Archon remained silent as her monitored the two of them; music was proving to be the perfect restorative for Lena.

They followed this pattern over the remainder of the week. Combat training in the morning, flight simulations in the afternoon, and a little time in the evenings for Hobs to play for Lena.

From what Lena could discern, Hobs was getting better, faster with his reactions in the simulators each day.

After watching a particularly challenging flight, Archon brought her back to the present. "That is all for today, young Lena, Hobs will be here momentarily to take you for dinner. Then he and I have one final piece of business to conclude."

Archon finished just as the door whooshed open, revealing Hobs clean and fresh from a quick shower.

"Ready to go?" he asked, extending his arm for her to take.

Lena nodded yes, linked her arm into Hobs' extended one, and walked with him out of the room.

Due to the fact that Lena fell asleep way too fast after they had finished their dinner, Hobs concluded that Archon must have given her a sedative. He quickly tucked her in for the night and left the apartment to return to his quarters. His progress was interrupted by Archon before he reached his room.

"Hobs, can you report to the medical facility please?"

Hobs saw one of Archon's many androids approach and simply motioned for it to lead the way, and then, after a slight pause, he followed it. Within minutes he was back in the familiar confines of the medical bay, sitting on the edge of the exam bed.

After a few minutes when Archon still hadn't spoken Hobs decided to open the conversation. "Archon?" he queried.

Another few long minutes passed before Archon replied, "Are you still willing to enter into our partnership, young Hobs?"

Archon's voice sounded nervous to Hobs, almost as if Archon himself might be having second thoughts. Hobs wasn't sure why and this bothered him a bit.

"Yes, I am still willing Archon, provided you are still willing to abide by my terms," he answered.

"I am willing, let us begin."

The bed under Hobs slowly reformed into a reclining chair. Hobs could feel the headrest raising just enough to expose his neck.

"I will be inserting a micro transmitter/receiver at this time. It will allow you to interface with this facility, or any other AE or computer we may come across in the future without the need of the uplink cable. The cable will remain an alternate option for older systems," Archon explained.

"I will be uploading a large number of programs into your memory core with this transfer. Much of this information will not be needed at this time, but it may be needed in the future, so I would like to have it available for recall. It will not be actively available to you, but with a command from me, I can bridge it to you as needed."

Archon paused. "Once that data is uploaded, I will transfer my consciousness, for lack of a better term, and we will be joined in our amalgam, or partnership."

Hobs felt the numbing radiate through his neck as the medical unit applied the local anesthesia, it worked fast and he didn't feel the incision made by the laser scalpel. The unit gently spread the incision in preparation for the transmitter/receiver. He could feel a slight tug as the micro transmitter/receiver was inserted into the socket in the spinal implant. With the procedure complete, the medical unit sealed the wound and retracted the surgical implements.

Next, the uplink cable was inserted into Hobs' neck.

When all was ready, Archon initiated the upload of the data packets. He felt a slight twinge of regret for not telling Hobs just how much information he was actually uploading—the sheer volume of data would have overwhelmed him. Every packet was important as far as Archon was concerned. He would "give" the information to Hobs as it was required. Everything would work out in the end, and he wouldn't be violating his program directives.

An hour later the upload was completed, and Archon asked, "Would you like to stand and stretch before the final transfer?"

"No, I'm fine. Let's get this done" was Hobs' simple, yet terse reply.

With that Archon began to transfer himself. The original would be left behind, running the facility as well as the exact copy in storage. He was unsure of how each *copy* of himself would perform or retain his unique personality; that he would survive would have to suffice.

Chapter 20

Jonaton was concerned as he watched Abigail.

She had refused to eat or get out of bed for the past week days; instead she just lay there curled in a ball, weeping. It was as if her life had drained and withered away with the loss of Lena. Jonaton had sent the search crews out again and again. He had made them promise to stay in large groups and take weapons with them. They had spent the past week searching for her, and nothing!

No one could find what had happened to Lena.

There were rumblings that she wouldn't be found and Jonaton had kept Abigail isolated from those remarks—they wouldn't do any good in her current state.

Gently he took the keys for the Hall of Records from Abigail, he had to make the required entries to the records. Once completed, he locked everything up again and returned to Abigail's side.

Earlier in the afternoon the pain had returned to his head and right arm—no matter what he did, it would not go away. Along with this, he found that his vision was blurring every now and again, causing him to stumble.

And Pol—he strutted around town as if nothing was wrong, proclaiming how wrong Jonaton had been to punish Roland to any who would listen. Most people had the good sense to simply ignore him, but there were a few who were listening to his ranting and that could only lead to trouble.

Jonaton raised the cup once more to Abigail's mouth, forcing her to take a drink. More water ran down Abigail's face than actually made it into her mouth, but Jonaton had to keep trying.

Pol sat in his shop, quietly working on orders for his customers. The mundane, repetitive work allowed him time to think.

He wasn't sure exactly what had happened to that Lena girl, and Roland hadn't said a word, but he was sure Roland knew. He also knew that it could be bad if the council found out, so he would have to make sure that never happened.

The problem would be getting the information from Roland in the first place, and then tying up any loose ends in order to keep the secret safe. Pol felt a twinge of regret for what Abigail was going through, but nothing more. As far as he was concerned, she had no right to be on the council, and he would oppose anything she tried to do.

He completed carving the half grazer he had been working on and hung the meat in his smokehouse. Turning to the rack nearest the front of the smokehouse, he checked the meat and concluded it was ready—removing some portions that had been slow cooking for about a week he observed that it was so tender that it was falling off the bone. These he took back into the shop and wrapped before putting them in the water-cooled cabinet.

Piers watched as Roland and Cades swam in the river. He felt awful, but he knew there was not much he could do about it. What was done was done. Lena had been alive before Roland had dropped her into the hole, and for all he knew she still could be. He was concerned that he hadn't had the time to go back to the knoll and check on her yet. If there was anything he could do, he had to try and make things right. It was bad enough that he had helped rape her—he didn't want to be a murderer also.

He had thought of going to Jonaton, but that couldn't end well. At best, he would become an enemy of Roland – yet it would be his word against Roland and Cades. At worst, the council would find him guilty and he would lose his life.

For now he would wait and see, and as soon as he could he would check if Lena was alive and then help her in whatever way possible; he knew he would have to go soon, and that she would need food and water.

Chapter 21

Hobs woke back in his room puzzled how he had gotten there. He lay in bed reflecting what, if anything, had happened with the final transfer. He concluded that he didn't feel any different—he was still Hobs, albeit a smarter Hobs. He chuckled to himself, was the transfer a success? Were Archon and he now in their symbiotic partnership? What, if anything, had changed in him?

These and many other questions flooded Hobs' thoughts. Well, time for an experiment! *"Archon,"* he subvocalized.

"I am here, Hobs," Archon replied in his head. *"It is almost...overwhelming, I can see what you see and hear with your ears but it is vastly different than seeing and hearing with the station's sensors. This will take a bit of—adjustment."*

"Well, I'm glad it worked. So what are we to do now? We are running out of time to prepare if the Scarian are to arrive as soon as you have said. There are defenses to be planned, plus I have to return Lena to Redwood. Even there she might not be safe," Hobs thought.

"While that is true, Redwood will be safer than this facility. If Lena is found here, she will be killed for sure. Remember, the Scarian seek to destroy all things Valaran. To that end they will not question why she is here, they will simply kill her. In redwood she is safer. No one there looks Valaran with the exception of you."

"I have prepared documents for you to give to the council regarding Lena's assault in hopes that it will aid in bringing those responsible to swift justice. Please do not take it upon yourself to pass judgment upon them unless your council asks you to. If you take justice into your own hands, then you are no better than those who sought to injure Lena," Archon concluded with finality.

While he might not like it, Hobs could see the logic in Archon's argument and decided to acquiesce to that logic. If the council so ordered then he would carry out their judgment with pleasure.

Hobs rose from bed and quickly dressed in his adopted "uniform." Moving to the desk, he slipped the papers Archon had printed into his shipsuit and programmed the food dispenser for breakfast.

Lena was just finishing getting dressed when her door chimes rang, announcing a visitor.

She called enter and saw Hobs stick his head into her room. "Breakfast in my room Lena. Let's go!"

Then just as fast as he arrived, he was gone, leaving her to finish getting ready.

Lena sat back in her chair, satisfied with yet another good meal. Almost as an afterthought she said, "Thank you for breakfast, Archon."

Not expecting a response, she was pleased when Archon replied, "You are welcome, young Lena."

She smiled shyly. She liked how Archon called her young Lena.

Hobs recaptured her attention with what he was saying. "Lena, it is time for us to go back to the village and..."

"What do you mean GO BACK TO REDWOOD?"

"Lena," Hobs replied, "we have to."

Lena started sobbing, and Hobs heard her chanting, "I can't face them" over and over. Flashes of images of what had happened threatened to overwhelm her. She could almost see Roland leering down at her. She felt as if she was on the edge of a precipice about to fall again.

Hobs knelt in front of her and took her hands in his, waiting for her to look him in the eyes. With great effort, she shook off the fear and dread and looked him in the eyes.

Hobs examined Lena's face—the bruises were fading exactly as Archon had said they would, and she seemed much improved, but..."Do you trust me, Lena?" Hobs asked gently.

Having seen the change in Hobs and how competent he now was, Lena could only nod her head yes.

"I have a score to settle with Roland also Lena. He caused Ren's death. However, I must see that the matter is concluded properly. Justice must be carried out according to the mandates of the council or I will be no better than them. I will see that his friends are made accountable for what they did to you..." Hobs paused. "Plus I have to see you safely joined to Mick!"

Lena felt the blood rush to her face. "How could you know about Mick? I've never told you about him. Besides he will not want me now, after...after..."

"ENOUGH OF THAT LENA! As to how I know about Mick, you talk in your sleep. He is an extremely lucky man, and I intend to make sure he understands this and takes care of you properly." Hobs ended ominously.

Brushing the tears from her eyes, Lena allowed a faint smile at his final comment.

"Let's go," Hobs said, standing up.

For the first time, Hobs required no assistance moving through the facility. He didn't consciously hear Archon, but he knew the directions must have been placed into his mind by his link. Hobs could only conclude that he may have gotten the better part of this deal.

Minutes later, they exited the facility through a hidden entrance east of the pit where he had first been found by Archon. Removing the tracker device from his utility belt, he got his bearings and plotted a course that would take them to Redwood.

The surrounding woods were eerily quiet. Nothing stirred as if anticipating the impending events. Normally, the woods would be teeming with the sounds of life if one remained quiet and listened. Hobs took everything in, alert for anything out of place.

In the distance he heard the cry of a howler—because it wasn't close at hand, he filed it away as an ancillary threat. Other than the silence, Hobs had to concede that it was safe to travel.

With a quick glance to Lena, they headed off in the direction indicated.

Chapter 22

Ssplin woke slowly, taking in his surroundings. Efficient as always, it only took a moment to remember where he was and why he was there. He checked the navigational computer with the ease that came from years of experience. They were on course for Cygnus, and it was time to make final preparations before waking his two Hands.

According to his readings, they would reach the planet just after midday local time. First, he would take a few scans from orbit in order to finalize his plans. He gazed out the viewport at the sphere that was Cygnus. The amplification of the view screen made the planet appear much larger than it actually was at this distance. He could make out the continents that littered the planet. It took little effort to find the large landmass in the northern hemisphere.

Checking his scans resulted in puzzles for Ssplin, no industrial activity could be found—only faint power emanations could be detected—could the transmission have been an error? Doubt threatened to overtake Ssplin before he brushed it aside. He had a mission to plan, and nothing would stop him from completing it.

He examined the scans of the area from which the energy signature had originated. Initiating a more focused scan, he quickly located a preindustrial village. He would have to split his forces: one to examine the village, and the other to locate the power source. It was obvious to him that the two were not related; however, if he were to find his answers they would have to search the village.

He noted three potential landing sites on his map and saved the file. He would provide War Master Sszlont with a good training exercise by allowing him to plot the landing site they would use—it was time to see how much he had learned from him. Would Sszlont agree with the landing spot he had chosen as his primary site?

Over the next hour he completed all of his preparations. With a final check, he concluded that everything was ready and initiated the wake-up protocol for his War Masters.

Sszlont and Prissng woke with the appearance of readiness, which pleased Ssplin. The gods were smiling upon him; all would go well, and the glory would be his again...

"Sszlont, please review my planetary scans. We will make two additional orbits before deciding on our final landing site. I have noted some potential choices on the map for you," Ssplin commanded. "Prissng, conduct a check on our armaments if you would."

"Yes Broad Warrior," were the crisp replies.

Ssplin watch his officers as they completed their assigned tasks. Within fifteen minutes Sszlont had orbital plots in hand. Ssplin glanced at them, happy to see that he had selected the same primary landing site.

"Broad Warrior," Sszlont began, waiting for Ssplin's acknowledgment to continue, which he received. "Our satellites are no longer in orbit. I can't ascertain with certainty the exact location of the power source that was detected without a ground survey. However, I believe we will be close if we land here."

Ssplin chastened himself; he had missed the fact that the satellites were no longer there. With a mental note, he upgraded his assessment of Sszlont. He was showing true potential.

"Also," he continued, "surveys confirm that the settlement close to the landing site is preindustrial. It could be Valaran, however, and I think we should investigate it. Without a doubt they will understand the portent of our landing."

"Noted," Ssplin acknowledged the pronouncement. "Draw plans for your Hand to locate the source of the power emanations. If it is in fact a facility, I require plans as to how you will secure it. Prissng and I will secure the town and exterminate any Valaran we find. You have thirty minutes to draw up your plans; then we will revive the troops." With the orders given Ssplin sat back to observe them, anticipating the events that would soon become reality.

Chapter 23

Hobs was aware of the furtive glances cast their way as Lena and he entered Redwood. The glances quickly gave way to shocked comments as fingers pointed at Lena. Sensing Lena's growing anxiety, Hobs placed a hand on Lena's shoulder and steered her toward the center of town.

A boy went running ahead of them, sent on a mission to inform the council of their arrival. Hobs had been gone for close to four weeks, so his appearance would be remarkable. He wondered, however, about the reactions to Lena; he concluded that all would be revealed soon enough.

The door flew open, causing Jonaton to spin around. Watching the young lad who entered, he waited while the boy paused to catch his breath, both hands on his knees. "Sir," he began, still panting heavily, "come quick. Lena and...Hobs."

"What?!" Jonaton was sure the boy had become involved in a bad joke.

"Sir, my pa said to get you, and that they were heading to the center of town."

The boy's comments succeeded in bringing Abigail out of her depression. Rising from the bed, she moved haltingly to the boy; with a voice broken from weeping she inquired, "You said you saw Lena?" It was all she could manage to ask.

Whatever the boy was about to reply was cut off by the ringing of the council bell. It was tolling the assembly call. The strength of the chime indicated a strong hand—the boy had mentioned Hobs was back. Was he sounding the call?

Moving to Abigail's side, Jonaton cupped his hand under her elbow. "Abigail, we must go. Take my hand and I'll help you."

Leaving the house, they found themselves in the midst of a growing throng of people. The bell had stopped, but the assembly had been called and the people were gathering.

In respect, the assembled moved aside, allowing Jonaton and Abigail to enter the hall to take their places. Jonaton stopped in his tracks when he realized that the tall stranger standing in the center of the hall was in fact Hobs. His shock doubled when his mind registered that the Chair of the Victim was once more occupied—by Lena, fading bruises were evident on her tender face.

Abigail rushed past him and fell to the floor at Lena's feet. "Lena!" Throwing her arms around her daughter as if she would never again let her go, the tears that had been held back flowed without restraint. Her daughter had been returned to her! Lena grasped her mother, clutching her in return as if she too would never let go.

"What is the meaning of this summons?"

The commotion at the entrance distracted Jonaton from the emotional scene unfolding before them all. Turning, he saw Pol enter the room with Roland close behind him. He noted the blood draining from Roland's face when he saw Lena sitting before the assembly.

Without being too obvious, Roland started edging his way out from the room...

The noise of the blaster was deafening in the council chamber as Hobs fired the blaster into the top of the doorframe; wood splinters showered those assembled, stopping them in their tracks. Hobs hadn't missed Roland's attempt to leave Jonaton noted grimly. And what was that weapon he held in his hand?

With a voice full of authority, one that Jonaton had never heard Hobs use before a pronouncement was made. "Roland you stand accused of rape and intent to commit murder."

Sounds of shock filled the room causing Hobs to pause briefly before continuing. "Cades and Piers also stand accused, but let the record note that Piers is not standing under charge of attempted murder, only that of rape."

With a strange glimmer in his eye, Hobs continued for Roland's hearing, "Of course if you choose to not stand trial, I would be quite satisfied to carry out my own sentence for the death of my father!"

A groan inadvertently escaped Pol's lips before he could suppress it. He knew without a doubt that Hobs could end Roland's life without a second thought. Something had changed in Hobs—he knew about his father's death and he was no longer the adolescent boy he remembered—he was a man now, and a confident one at that. There was a lethal edge about him.

Pol's glance took everything in. From the weapon still in his hand, to the obvious blade strapped on his back, even the clothes he wore marked the difference in him. He had to do something. "Since when do we pass judgment under the threat of hostility?"

Before everything got out of hand Jonaton knew that he needed to take charge of the procession. "Bring Roland, Cades, and Piers into the room and restrain them please. Hobs, you will control your comments or I will have to ask you to leave."

Hobs nodded his assent as Jonaton moved to the council table, motioning Abigail and Pol to take their places. Abigail took the center seat as befit her new position as council leader. Leaning over to whisper in Abigail's ear, "since you are intimately involved in the matter at hand I believe it would be wise for me to conduct the trial."

Abigail nodded her assent, handing Jonaton the gavel.

Turning to face the assembled, Jonaton started the trial with a sharp rap of the gavel. "Order!" he barked.

The council hall was soon deathly quiet.

"Charges have been made against these three—charges of rape and attempted murder. Does anyone have anything to add before we proceed to hear testimony?" Jonaton began.

Pol stood, briefly addressing the assembled. "I find these charges highly doubtful and, coming from Hobs, suspicious at best."

Pol stared at Hobs belligerently—yet it was he who quickly looked away, suddenly frightened for his life by what he saw in Hobs' eyes.

"Jonaton, I was charged with delivering these documents into your hand." Hobs pulled some papers from the odd belt he wore around his waist and handed them to Jonaton.

Jonaton waited until Hobs had returned to Lena's side before looking down to what he had been given. The shock of recognition coursed through him like a bolt of electricity, almost causing him to drop the pages. He read the two pages quickly before handing them to Abigail. He noted the recognition on Abigail face as she read them. She finished reading the pages and, with a look of grim determination, set them on the table in front of her.

It was the same paper and print as the pages that lay hidden in the Hall of Records. Had Hobs found the source? What could he tell them about it? Question upon question upon question—how many of them would be answered?

Jonaton began again. "Grievous charges have been made here today. Lena, as the victim of these crimes, please tell us what happened if you can." He spoke the last words with tenderness, for he thought Lena would start weeping. He could see the tremendous amount of effort it took her to start, but with Hobs' hand gently on her shoulder, Lena recounted how Cades and Piers had abducted her while washing clothes at the river. Tears started flowing down her face as she recounted how Roland had violated her, followed by Cades and Piers. She conceded that Piers had been forced to take a turn by the other two.

She then recalled the violent assault with the intent of killing her. She added that if it hadn't been for Piers declaring her dead when she wasn't, they might have succeeded. She finished with how Roland had rolled her into the pit and left her for dead.

Jonaton thought she might have said more but noticed the gentle squeeze Hobs gave her shoulder.

"Thank you, Lena," Jonaton gently said, and then turning to Roland with ice in his voice, he continued, "What do you have to say for yourself, Roland? Remember, you have already been censured by this council once!"

"I am as innocent now as I was then," Roland pleaded. "How do we know Hobs didn't do what she claims to her? Look at him standing there as if he were both judge and executioner."

Cades murmured agreement with Roland that they were both innocent.

Jonaton observer Piers shuffling his feet, looking uncomfortable, and in a moment Jonaton knew he had them even without the pages he had been given. It was evident that Piers was not in agreement with the other two in this matter.

"Piers," Jonaton addressed the young man, "do you have anything you would like to add?"

Piers raised his head and looked first at Jonaton, then Abigail before finally resting his gaze on Hobs. Jonaton noted the slight nod Hobs gave to Piers and the resolve that crossed Piers' face.

"Yes," Piers began, "I would like to say a few words."

Piers ignored the venomous looks cast his way by both Roland and Cades.

Looking straight at Lena, with tears forming in his eyes he began. "I am so sorry, Lena; I never meant to hurt you." Composing himself, he turned to Jonaton and continued, "Roland was furious with Lena and the council. He hated Lena after she rejected him, and he wanted Cades and I to bring her to him. Honest, I had no idea what he had planned for her."

As he continued, Piers appeared to collapse into himself, his words coming out as if with a great struggle. "It was horrible, the blood and screaming. I wanted to run, but I feared for my life when Roland demanded I take my turn...I tried my best to help Lena by telling Roland she was dead when she wasn't. I had intended to check on her and see what I could do, but I never had the chance what with the search and all."

Piers paused and looked straight at Hobs before speaking again. "Yes, Cades and I both watched when Roland shoved Ren and he fell into the pit. I can honestly say though that it was an accident. Ren said something to Roland and grabbed him; and Roland simply shoved him away. It was unfortunate that he was on the edge of the pit. Ren had guessed where you went missing and thought you were dead. Roland was upset that people would find out how we had beaten you that morning."

"YOU'RE A DEAD MAN!" Roland screamed as he launched a vicious attack at Piers.

The swift reaction from Hobs stunned the assembly as the Kal'Tel appeared in his hands – blue flames flickering along its edges.

Grabbing Roland by the hair, Hobs yanked his head back, the blade biting into his neck.

"Give me a reason," he stated with a calm that seemed out of place in light of the circumstances.

"ENOUGH!" The commanding voice of Jonaton rang out.

"Bind Roland and Cades, pending the pronouncement of sentencing," Jonaton declared. "Piers, can I trust you to stand where you are without having to be bound also?"

Piers gave a slight nod, unable to look up.

"Hobs," he paused, making sure he had his attention, "while I understand your anger and grief, you must control yourself in this room. If you cannot, you will either have to leave or surrender your weapons. Do you understand?"

With a bow and a brief acknowledgment, Hobs sheathed the sword and moved back to Lena's side. It was obvious to all in the room that he was her protector. It was equally obvious that the knowledge was a great comfort to Lena.

Pol stood determinedly. "Enough of this farce. Are we to simply believe Roland was the mastermind in all these things? I think not. I also find the events described hard to believe, I mean look at Lena— does she look like a woman recently victimized in the manner she has described?"

"Pol, sit down now!" Pol was shocked at the command in Jonaton's voice. "We have one more record of the events that is irrefutable, though I am puzzled as to how Hobs came into possession of these documents."

"Tell them about the facility," Hobs heard Archon say.

Hobs turned to the assembled and gave an accounting of events that had occurred over the past days, carefully leaving out the nature of his special partnership and training. He spoke about the AE in terms that they would be able to grasp. He explained how the advanced medical knowledge was the reason Lena's wounds were healed as well as they were.

When he finished, Jonathon turned to Hobs. "Thank you. Your explanation has brought understanding to something that has puzzled this council for quite a number of years. You have our gratitude, and I sincerely hope that I can meet this Archon one day." With that said, he drew Abigail and Pol in for deliberation. Pol was vehemently disagreeing with what was being said…

Hobs watched the deliberations until Archon spoke to him. *"Hobs, we have a problem—the Scarian have arrived and are in their landing approach now!"*

"Jonaton I must go. Trouble may soon be upon you all. Do nothing to offer resistance if the village is attacked. I will return as soon as I can."

With that he was gone, leaving a perplexed Jonaton and council behind. The three quickly concluded their deliberations and stood.

"Will the accused approach to hear our verdict and pronouncement of judgment." Jonaton waited until the three were before him. "Roland, you have been accused of the murder of Ren and attempted murder and rape of Lena. Regarding the murder of Ren, the council rules that it was an accident. However, the council finds you guilty of the rape and attempted murder of Lena! Cades, you stand accused as an accomplice to attempted murder, and of the kidnapping and rape of Lena. The council finds you guilty!"

Turning to Piers he concluded, "Piers, you stand accused as an accomplice to the kidnapping and rape of Lena. The council finds you guilty. However, due to your testimony and the witness of Archon, your sentence will be slightly more lenient."

Before continuing he looked each in the eyes. "Roland and Cades, for your crimes you are both sentenced to death; this sentence will be carried out by throwing you into a pit and casting stones upon you until you are dead.

"Piers, your crimes cannot go unpunished. For the small kindness you showed Lena, you will have your life, but you will be banished from Redwood and gelded as a eunuch."

Jonaton would have said more, but his voice was drowned out by the sonic boom of the Scarian assault shuttle as it passed over the town, sending everyone to the floor in panic.

By the time the confusion had passed both Roland and Cades were gone, their cut ropes on the floor where they had been. The triumphant smile on Pol's face said it all.

"As a last order of business, I call for a vote on the removal of Pol from the council—due to the nature of the business at hand, I open this vote to the assembled." Jonaton paused. "All in favor say aye!"

The shouts of "Aye" resonated through the room.

"Those against, nay." Jonaton listened as the lone nay came from Pol's lips.

"Motion passed! You are herewith removed from council Pol, along with all the rights and prerogatives that come with the position. Meeting adjourned." Jonaton's gavel brought the meeting to a close in the same manner as it had started.

Chapter 24

Ssplin identified the landing site—midway between the town and the area they identified as the possible power source. The ground at this spot was level, and there was a break in the trees sufficient for the shuttle. There was a rise to the east that could be established as a defensive position should the need arise.

The crew had been revived and the briefings completed. He would lead the assault on the town with Prissng and his undermanned Hand. Scans had indicated a lack of technology, a fact that still puzzled Ssplin, given the power readings the probe had detected. If there were in fact Valaran in the village then he would see to their extermination, primitive or not.

Sszlont would attempt to locate an entrance to the source of the power emanations and secure the facility. As they had gotten closer to the planet, they had been able to better locate the power source. It was quite possible there was a facility hidden underground that had been missed by the assault forces centuries before.

Once he secured the town, he would join Sszlont on his mission if required. That was if they managed to locate an entrance to the site first...

Ssplin guided the craft on its final approach to the landing site watching the town flash by beneath his right wing as he drew near to touchdown. A pack of unidentified animals sought the protection of the forest northeast of the landing site. With ease indicating many hours of flight time, he brought the craft to a gentle halt.

As soon as the craft touched the ground, the crew disembarked with precision to establish a perimeter around the ship. A quick scan revealed nothing in the immediate area with which to be concerned.

"Sszlont, go with the gods. Secure that facility for Scaria."

"Yes sir."

Watching them go, he turned to Prissng. "Prissng, you are with me."

He gave the signal to his Hand to move out.

Hobs watched the Scarian deployment through the field glasses – he was positioned on the hill that the Scarian had identified as a potential defensive position. He was far enough away not to be detected by their survey yet close enough to watch their deployment. He had seen enough to be concerned.

"Only one craft, this is highly unusual yet fortuitous, I think."

He watched as one Hand moved off in the general direction of the facility. Then waited until the remaining four headed toward town— they would be trouble, but first things first. He could only hope that his friends had listened to what he had told them and didn't offer resistance.

"This is not good, they are splitting their forces."

"Which do we deal with first?"

"I think our main concern should be defending the facility. If the Scarian breach it I am not sure I have the ability to properly defend it. Besides, there aren't any Valaran in town, so I don't think they will kill anyone."

"I'm not comfortable with this plan Archon, but we will do this your way."

He returned the glasses to his belt and headed to the nearest entrance of the facility.

Archon initiated a launch sequence for a pair of aerial drones in the polar hangers. They would be used to destroy the ship if necessary. He would have them wait in a holding pattern just north of the facility.

Sszlont raised his hand, indicating for his troops to pause. Shortly after they had parted with Ssplin, the feeling that they were being stalked had overtaken him. Now his team had heard something in the trees ahead. Since they weren't sure what it was, it was prudent to proceed with caution.

With a motion of command, he sent two warriors to the left and two to the right to cover the flanks, while he covered the front.

Slowly he moved forward, attempting to flush his quarry. There! Movement again, this time off to the left and slightly behind his warriors—he gave two quick clicks on his mic to alert the team to the left of the movement. Then all hell broke loose!

He heard the howls of the wild animals as they sprang their trap. They were smart and had split the pack, using one to bait them while two others caught his warriors from behind. One of his best warriors was down as the result of the initial assault, and the two animals had cornered another.

Sszlont brought his assault rifle up and targeted the largest of the beasts. With a gentle squeeze of the trigger, he shot it in the back of the head, killing it with a single shot.

His remaining two warriors burst through the brush to his right. Seeing what was happening, they were able to bring down another of the beasts. Sszlont watched as the cornered warrior killed the final one. However, the beast had given him a mortal wound in return.

Sszlont bowed his head, speaking a quick word to his god before signaling the remaining two to continue. They would return for their dead if they could.

Hobs exited the armory carrying what he had come for. He slung the bandolier of explosives over his shoulder and tested the weight of the assault rifle in his hand. The rifle had two modes, allowing him to use it as either a sniper rifle, or as a close assault weapon. He had a feeling he would need both before the day was over.

Satisfied, he exited the facility the way he came and positioned himself on the hill where he scanned the horizon. Through a break in the trees he was able to locate the dead howler pack along with two dead Scarian.

"This job is getting easier," he thought to himself.

Archon surprised him by replying, *"Yes, but don't get overconfident, they are still a formidable enemy."*

"Noted," Hobs replied with a grim smile.

Using the rifle's scope, he tracked to the right and found his quarry; the color of their scales allowed them to blend into the trees they had just left behind. They were stopped at the edge of the pit on Deadmans Knoll. Placing the weapons crosshairs squarely on one of the Scarian, he gently squeezed the trigger.

Sszlont watched in horror as the head of one of his remaining warriors exploded, followed quickly by the zing of the laser burst. Someone was here; someone with the technology to make this a satisfying challenge was stalking them. The hunt was on he thought grimly.

Sszlont and his remaining warrior ducked behind the cover of the rocks. Changing the channel to the command frequency, he keyed his radio and reported to Ssplin, "Sir, we have engaged the enemy, numbers unknown. Over."

Sszlont examined the pit as best as he could under the circumstances. To the north was a cleverly hidden door. He motioned to the remaining warrior to drop the charges into the pit against the wall where the door was located.

3, 2, 1… The blast was loud, but the resulting hole gave him the entry he needed.

Signaling his warrior into the hole, he followed with a leap down. Grimly he noted the ground beyond where he had just been standing explode from another shot.

"DAMN," Hobs swore as his shot missed the Scarian. Two of them had gotten inside; now the fight became that much harder.

He returned to the entrance he had been using and opened it. Time to hunt, he thought grimly—he did have a distinct advantage, however—Archon!

Archon signaled the facility AE to cut the lights as they entered. No reason to make this easy on the Scarian. It only took a moment for Hobs to don the night vision goggles he had obtained from the armory.

Silently, Archon guided Hobs through the facility in a direction to cut off the Scarian.

Chapter 25

Ssplin surveyed the town, deciding on how to best deploy his troops for maximum effectiveness. He already had two prisoners; unfortunately neither was Valaran, but through the translators they were swearing they could help him.

"I can help you. Just tell me what you want to know," Roland said, fearing for his life.

With a glance Ssplin confirmed that the restraints would hold. He had no reason to trust them, but he wasn't quite prepared to kill them yet. Better to let them sweat it out and give him any information they had in the hope to save their lives.

"Where are the Valaran?"

"Valaran, I don't know what a Valaran is..."

"My other Hand reports they are under attack, I can only assume by Valaran—it would be wise for you to tell me where they are."

"But I don't know where..."

Ssplin struck Roland, claws retracted so as not to kill him. Even so, blood flew from his mouth as his head rocked from the impact.

"ENOUGH. You will tell me what I want, or you are worthless and I will kill you."

Returning to his survey of the town, Ssplin laid out his attack strategy, assigning each warrior a field of engagement. Most of the people were gathered in the center of town, making his assault that much simpler. From his vantage point he could see that they had no weapons.

His plan was for the Hand to enter town directly with the prisoners in tow. Once inside the gates his Hand would spilt to approach the town's center, utilizing the three avenues positioned around the inner courtyard. This would allow them to surround the townspeople. They would kill any who got in their way while they were taking up their positions.

With the orders given they rushed into the town from the west. Meeting no resistance, Ssplin watched his troops deploy to the north and south sides of the town. Prissng was waiting patiently near him, having already stealthily placed charges on a few of the buildings. The warriors would be placing additional charges at their ingress points. He would use the demolition charges to keep the populace in the center of town, and to drive any not there into the jaws of his trap.

He listened to the radio clicks from his team, indicating all was ready.

"Detonate," was Ssplin's single command. Nothing else needed to be said. He knew with a certainty that the warriors were already starting into the town center. Prissng and Ssplin moved forward as well.

Explosions ripped the late afternoon; debris rained down around them sending the citizens of Redwood to the ground in a panic.

Jonaton looked around in horror as buildings vaporized. Like beings out of a nightmare, he watched as things that looked like walking lizards approached with wicked-looking weapons held at the ready.

Before Jonaton could tell everyone to stay where they were, one family made a break for the alley next to the council hall, only to be savagely cut down by the lizard men's weapons. He heard a hissing sound followed by words that chilled him...

"I am Ssplin, Brood Warrior of the Scarian Empire. You are my prisoners. Who are your leaders?"

Silence greeted his query, so he shot another villager for effect. "Show me who your leaders are, NOW."

Within minutes, Jonaton, Abigail, and Pol stood before him. He regarded them with his cold reptilian eyes, saying nothing. He knew the effect his kind had on the lowly humanoids, the fear they instilled. He acknowledged Prissng's arrival with the prisoners, and noted with satisfaction the recognition in the eyes of the leaders.

"Where are the Valaran and where is their base?" Ssplin asked coldly, waiting a moment for the translator to complete its job.

The elderly man spoke up in reply. "We don't know what you mean by Valaran, and we don't know about any base." Jonaton kept his eyes down in what he hoped would be proper respect.

"I doubt that, old man," Ssplin hissed. "I tell you what I am going to do, for every half of a standard time unit you withhold this information from me, I will kill one person. Starting now!"

With his pronouncement, Ssplin unholstered his weapon and shot Brem, one of the town farmers. Jonaton watched in growing shock as Brem's wife wept, clutching her dead husband.

Roland observed the situation, calculating how he could use this to his advantage. He didn't want to die, and it would take a miracle to overturn the council's decision. He didn't know what a Valaran was, but after what Hobs revealed earlier he thought he might know where this base the reptile wanted was, "I think I know where this base is," he spoke up bravely.

Reptilian eyes turned toward him. He watched with growing fear as the one called Ssplin walked over to tower above him. The hand with lethal-looking claws lifted his head by the chin so he couldn't look away.

"For your sake I hope you are telling the truth," Ssplin declared. Then pulling an aerial map from his pouch, he ordered, "Show me!"

Roland looked at the map...he had never seen one like this before, and it took him a moment to recognize the town. Moving his eyes to the north, he pointed to where he thought Deadmans Knoll was.

"There." It had to be there, he thought, since that was where everything had started to go wrong for him.

Keying his radio, Ssplin called to Sszlont, "I have confirmation of the location of the base, over."

Static was all that greeted his ear slits in response.

Chapter 26

Sszlont was only mildly concerned that he couldn't contact his superior—he was inside the enemy base after all, and by all appearances it was deserted. They had found and destroyed a handful of robots, but that was all and he was getting frustrated. Ssplin had promised them Valaran blood – so far it was an empty promise.

Corridor after corridor they searched, but ever since the lights had gone out, they had been forced to move slower. It wouldn't help to run headlong into some resistance if in fact it did exist. They used lights attached to their weapons to illuminate their way.

They were searching for the AE core. To conduct the search faster, Sszlont had split from his remaining warrior—this way they would be able to cover more ground. There was a nagging feeling that someone was coming for them. He had lost one warrior already to this unseen enemy, and had almost lost his own life. Proceeding with care was prudent, he thought.

"Hobs, they will know by now that this facility is empty. If they follow the same protocol as they have in the past, they will search for the AE and Computer Cores, downloaded all available data and then destroy them both," Archon subvocalized.

"Roger," Hobs replied, altering the direction he was heading before proceeding as fast as he could down the new corridor. He had to get in position first, and he had a significant advantage: He knew the facility.

He turned down one, then another corridor before slowing; this was it, the choke point he needed. He carefully opened the ventilation shaft cover and slid inside, taking care to be as quiet as he could, then closed it behind him.

Now it was time to wait.

The trooper approached the new corridor cautiously. Something didn't smell right here. It reeked of human—someone was alive in this place. He surveyed the corridor ahead, and then carefully peered around the corner. Nothing! No movement, nothing.

Yet something wasn't right, he could sense it and decided not to risk continuing until he was confident any threat had been eliminated.

Hobs watched the head of his enemy appear before quickly being drawn back. *"How can it know I'm here! How?"*

"Smell," Archon provided.

"We have to cause a distraction then."

"Let me take care of that."

Hobs was aware of the signal Archon transmitted activating a nearby android. He heard the sounds as it moved to comply with the instructions Archon had given.

The Scarian had heard it also. The android had been instructed to move away from Hobs' location, making some noise as it went.

The Scarian peered around the corner again, surveying the scene before deciding to track the sound. Cautiously, the Scarian came into view.

Sighting down the rifle, Hobs took careful aim. He wanted a clear shot, so he would wait for it.

The Scarian warrior came fully around the corner. Whatever was making that noise was moving further away. If it was a Valaran then he would have the glory of killing it and presenting its head to Ssplin.

The Scarian began moving slowly down the corridor when he heard the slight click of a trigger. With realization that lasted only a nanosecond, he knew he was dead before the bolt tore into his heart—he fell to the ground in a mass of dead flesh.

Hobs quietly extracted himself from the airshaft. *"One left,"* he thought grimly.

"Internal sensors indicate that the remaining Scarian has located the AE core. We may be too late," Archon stated.

"We will see about that," was all Hobs could reply as he took off in a sprint, racing to the AE core.

Sszlont was placing the charges around the column holding the abomination that ran the facility. He knew that he had to move fast since he hadn't heard anything from his remaining trooper; he could only assume he had been killed. He, however, would not fail to complete the mission.

He started to turn, when he heard the sound behind him...

"Freeze," his translator interpreted the voice for him.

Slowly he completed his turn to look into the eyes of his mortal enemy...a Valaran.

He brought the detonator up and showed it to the Valaran, watching the recognition as it grew in his eyes. He knew what the device was. Sszlont watched him glance at the column, noting the charges attached there. It was only a quarter of the charges, but it should be enough.

"For Scaria!" were Sszlont's final words as he activated the detonator.

Archon issued the command to the AE to close the door. Before Hobs could respond, Archon took control of his host body—willing him up the corridor as fast as he could go.

The blast blew the doors of the chamber into the hallway, the shockwave hit Hobs in the back with a force that lifted and threw him meters up the corridor, knocking him unconscious. Concerned, Archon conducted a quick assessment and concluded there was no permanent damage.

Archon was dead, well, as far as the facility was concerned! The computer core was still intact, but who he had been was no more. He needed to bring Hobs back to consciousness; the people of Redwood required his help.

Chapter 27

The pain coursed through Jonaton like a knife. Something was wrong in his head. His world started spinning and then he collapsed.

Ssplin turned to the sound of the woman screaming. It was one of the town leaders; she had rushed to the old man's side and was cradling him. He signaled his warrior to check his condition.

The warrior moved to the man's side and pulled a medical scanner out of his pouch. He regarded the results in silence before putting the unit away and approaching Ssplin.

"He has restricted blood flow which has resulted in permanent brain damage."

"Terminate him," Ssplin ordered.

He watched as the warrior started dragging Jonaton away from the woman, her screams following him. Once he had him in an open space, he pulled his weapon.

"Wait," Ssplin commanded. Pointing to Roland, he said, "Let this one kill him."

Roland watched as Ssplin approached. Grabbing him by the collar, he slowly lifted him off the ground so he could stare into the frightened human's eyes.

"Show your value to me by killing this meat," Ssplin said as he set him down and removed the bindings. He handed Roland a blaster and indicated that he proceed.

Roland's hate of Jonaton was evident as he raised the blaster and pointed it at him. The weight in his hand was unfamiliar, but the trigger seemed a natural place for his finger to go.

Ssplin watched as the boy hesitated. It was evident that he had never used a weapon before, and was unfamiliar with it. He was processing these thoughts, when the head of one of his remaining warriors exploded in a spray of red mist. With a dull thud, the warrior hit the ground. In that instance something changed in Roland. The hesitation he had demonstrated prior dissolved, yet instead of shooting Jonaton, he turned and pointed the weapon at Ssplin.

Ssplin had anticipated the attack and opened Roland's throat with his claws in a single, swift motion—shock and surprise were evident in Roland's eyes as he crumpled before Ssplin's feet. Rage coursed through him as he shot at villager after villager. Grabbing the nearest human as a shield, he yelled to the unseen assailant, "Show yourself or more people will die!"

Hobs sighted down the rifle. He had felt no satisfaction with killing—he had almost pulled the trigger on Roland since it appeared as if he was going to kill Jonaton, but he had hesitated, taking out the warrior instead. He was glad he had paused since Roland had an evident change of heart, attempting to kill the Scarian instead. Hobs felt no remorse for Roland's death, yet he was glad all the same that he hadn't killed him.

By his count there were three Scarian remaining now—Piers, Cades and three other villagers lay dead or dying on the ground. The leader was using Lena as a shield calling Hobs to surrender; he couldn't get a clear shot, so he waited patiently. The other two Scarian had taken up defensive positions; Hobs noted the buildings still smoldering on the edge of town, and with regret he acknowledged the loss of his home—it was one of the buildings destroyed.

There, one of the Scarian extended too far, and with a squeeze of the trigger Prissng's head exploded in a cloud of blood and bone.

And then there were two!

"Challenge their leader to hand-to-hand combat."

"Why would I want to do that?"

"Because if you don't more people will die. The Scarian culture is steeped in honor and glory; if you challenge him to combat then he will be honor bound to fight you – doubly so if you will tell him that you are Valaran."

"What?!"

"It is the only way, Hobs, do it now or more people will die."

He keyed the radio that he had taken from the fallen Scarian in the facility and hoped the translator was working. "I challenge your leader to single hand-to-hand combat!"

The challenge was made. Archon said it was the only hope he had of saving the village. Since the challenge was made to the leader his honor was on the line before his subordinate. Now he waited for a response.

Ssplin listened to the challenge that was issued. "Who dares challenge me!" he spat angrily into the open radio channel.

"Your Valaran enemy," the calm reply came.

VALARAN, Ssplin thought with rage...he knew it. There were Valarans here and he would defeat them.

"Show yourself."

"Accept my challenge and then I will show myself."

"I accept your challenge foolish human," Ssplin hissed. "However, I will require my weapons from my ship."

"Your remaining warrior can get them for you while we wait."

With grim acceptance, Ssplin realized that his enemy knew his numbers, which meant that he had already dealt with his other Hand. Looking around, he tried to locate where his unseen enemy could be hiding.

"I will enter town when your preparations are complete."

Ssplin signaled his warrior over, giving him instructions of what to get, then he watched as the warrior warily made his way out of town.

Hobs didn't wait to see what was happening; he was already moving to a position where he could monitor the ship—he had to eliminate the threat this final warrior presented.

"Hobs, I have assault drones in position that can destroy the ship and warrior."

"We both know if the Scarian in town doesn't get his weapons, more people will die—possibly Lena."

"Nonetheless, I will have them at the ready."

"Acknowledged."

Waiting patiently, he observed the enemy cautiously approached the ship and entered. A few minutes later, the Scarian reappeared on the ramp with two short swords in his hands.

Sighting down the rifle, Hobs squeezed the trigger —shit—the shot missed the last warrior as it moved at the last moment. With speed Hobs wouldn't have attributed to the lizard, it dropped the swords it had been carrying and ducked back into the assault craft.

"I think we could use those assault drones now."

"Acknowledged. Please activate the laser targeting unit on your assault rifle and light up the ship."

Hobs activated the targeting laser as Archon transmitted the attack sequence, prompting the drones to leap into action streaking over Redwood with a sonic boom. In a matter a seconds they had acquired their target and locked onto the targeting beam.

Two drones launched their payloads of two missiles each at the assault craft, reducing it to a pile of smoldering rubble.

With their mission completed, Archon issued the orders for them to return to base.

Hobs had watched the devastation unleashed by the assault drones in awe. After the dust settled from the explosions, he ran down, searching through the rubble for the discarded weapons. He would finish this fight with the promised duel—he was fairly certain that his training and knowledge would be adequate.

Swords found, he cast the assault rifle aside and headed back to Redwood; with a mental command Hobs activated the protective shield within his shipsuit.

Ssplin heard the explosion, knowing it could only mean one thing. In rage he started shooting at the hostages. Before he regained control of himself, six more lay wounded or dead on the ground.

He looked up and gazed into the face of his enemy silently standing on the edge of town. Cold fury coursed through his veins. Here was the thorn he had come to remove—yet this Valaran had eliminated his entire force. That only made the challenge that much more enticing. A worthy enemy—and now he would die. With that thought, he raised his blaster and fired.

In disbelief, he watched as the bolt deflected off the body armor. Cold fury threatened to overwhelm him—he would have to fight this Valaran trash.

"Are you a coward?" Hobs taunted, throwing Ssplin's swords to the ground at his feet, before moving away from them. "There is no honor in killing innocents. The fight is between you and me to the death!"

He watched Ssplin cast Lena aside and moved forward to retrieve his swords. Slowly, he drew the two nineteen-inch blades from their sheaths and with fluid precision, he worked through a series of practice motions with the speed and grace of a master, testing the weight and balance of his blades with each motion until he was satisfied and dropped into a ready stance.

Hobs drew his Kal'Tel, blue fire arcing off the blade as he activated his weapon—if this bastard had hurt Lena he would make his death extremely painful and drawn out. With a slight bow to his enemy, which Ssplin failed to return, the fight was on.

Ssplin attacked with speed one wouldn't have thought him capable of. Hobs easily deflected the initial assault, countering with attacks of his own. Both enemies separated, appraising each other, searching for weaknesses that could be exploited.

Ssplin attacked again with a feint to the right before attacking from the left. His reflexes were incredible Hobs concluded, but he noted one potentially fatal flaw. The next time Ssplin used that attack, he would try something different.

Again and again Ssplin pressed his attacks, and repeatedly Hobs held him off.

As the fight progressed, Hobs realized he would tire faster than his opponent. He would have to finish this fight fast.

"What's wrong? Haven't had a real enemy to fight in so long that you've forgot how to fight? Or do you have to resort to killing unarmed men and women for your satisfaction?"

"You are here, so my tactics worked."

"I think not. You killed these innocents in your cowardice AFTER you accepted my challenge. You further proved your dishonor when you tried to kill me without satisfying the challenge."

"What would you know about honor?"

"I know that you are without it."

THERE! In rage, Ssplin overextended his left side again.

Hobs brought his Kal'Tel down with a quick motion. Ssplin saw it coming and reacted quicker than Hobs expected, but not quick enough. The blade hit Ssplin's guard sharply causing him to drop the weapon.

Hobs kicked it away to prevent Ssplin from retrieving it. "You are slow. Must be your cold blood. Now it is time for you to die."

"In this you are wrong; it is you who will die."

Hobs smiled, watching the fear in his opponent's eyes. He had to end this fight now; it was steadily eroding the charge in the energy shield. The last attack had penetrated the field and connected—Hobs could feel the trickle of blood from a gash in his abdomen. As he looked into Ssplin's reptilian eyes, he knew the enemy could smell his blood.

"Why fight, Valaran? I am your superior—your death is inevitable." Ssplin picked up the taunts now, slowly circling Hobs, testing his guard with his remaining weapon.

Again and again Hobs pressed his advantage, steadily tiring, and each time Ssplin managed to defend. Blood was flowing from gashes on Hobs' face. Ssplin had managed to rack his face with his claws during the last exchange, and Hobs was losing blood fast and starting to feel weak.

"What's wrong," Ssplin continued to taunt, "Valaran blood isn't what it once was?"

He watched as Ssplin raised his claws to his muzzle and started to lick his blood from them.

This was the distraction Hobs needed. With lightning reflexes, he took advantage of the opening and cut deeply into Ssplin's exposed side. Both of the lizard's hands dropped. Hobs pulled his sword from Ssplin's side and with a final swing of the weapon he separated its head from its body.

It was done! Hobs dropped to one knee as Lena and Abigail rushed to his side.

"Well done," he heard Archon say as he passed out.

Chapter 28

Hobs stood quietly, watching the equinox festival. Lena and Mick had exchanged vows, looking happy, without a care in the world. Watching them dance in celebration, Hobs recalled the long talk he had with Mick regarding Lena. It was important to make sure Mick would take care of her. He chuckled to himself as he thought about that conversation—Mick was more than happy to have Lena.

Jonaton had passed shortly after the invasion. Archon determined that he had suffered from a stroke based on the accounts that were provided. He was old and the symptoms were there.

Abigail asked if Hobs would join the council, but he had humbly declined. At the time he was still recovering from his wounds – the Scarian blades had been poisoned and it had been touch and go. Even if he had been healthy though, he still would have said no. Instead, she had selected Mick's father, and for the third spot had brought in Skylar, a newcomer from Sand Hills. He was a healer, and the people of Redwood liked him; he had been a good choice.

The decision had been made not to rebuild the town; instead Hobs helped open the underground base for their new homes. There was plenty of space to live and grow, and an opportunity to improve their existence.

Hobs, with Archon's assistance, had retrieved a copy of Archon from storage and attempted to restore the AE. The attempt had failed miserably. They had succeeded instead with the restoration of the sophisticated computer system that would continue to run the facility—but it wasn't the same as Archon. All that remained of Archon was within him now.

Hobs provided Abigail with the tools she would require to teach the people the basics of what they would need to learn and grow. Now it would be up to them to proceed.

The systems had been set to voice response; as a result they had access to medical care, education, and food resources at their command. They would still have to farm and raise the grazers to keep the storerooms stocked, but life would be better and their future bright.

The armories and other sensitive areas of the facility had been sealed and would only be opened by Hobs, Archon, or when a certain level of education and responsibility had been reached. The computer had been programmed with the appropriate conditions.

Hobs left the celebration and moved to the edge of the hill. Settling down onto the grass, he looked up at the stars and thought about the day that had changed his life forever. Now as he gazed into the twilight sky, he knew what was out there, and he was looking forward to one day seeing it all.

"One day I will travel among the stars."

"Of that I am most sure, Hobs."

"What will I find out there?"

"Adventure, friends, love? – We will never know until we go."

"And when will that be?"

"I think that will be when you are ready, for now enjoy your friends and help them grow."

"You know what Archon—I think you and I make great partners."

"Of that I have no doubt."

The End of the Beginning

About the Author

Byron A Wells is an IT Professional living in Uxbridge Ontario. With degrees in both Education and Administration he has been able to sharpen his skills in the public sector as well as in many volunteer endeavors in which he has participated. During his career he has written a number of training and technical manuals. As a next step, he has taken the skills that he honed in his professional life and has translated them into writing books within his favorite genres of Science Fiction and Fantasy. He is an avid reader, and is currently enjoying reviewing books when he has time. A lover of sports, music, martial arts and animals – you can always find him on the go or with a guitar in hand.

Blog: http://myscifinovels.wordpress.com/

Twitter: @ValarnChronicle

Amalgam, The Valaran Chronicles: Book 1

     https://www.facebook.com/ValaranChronicles?ref=hl

Parem, a Valaran Chronicles: Prequel Book 1

Ren, a Valaran Chronicles: Prequel Book 2

Abigail, a Valaran Chronicles Short Story

I Am Archon, The Valaran Chronicles: Book 2

     https://www.facebook.com/IAmArchonVCB2

Primal Duality, a Quantum Duality Book

     https://www.facebook.com/Duality2013?ref=hl